I Met Loh Kiwan

MODERN KOREAN FICTION

Bruce Fulton, General Editor

TREES ON A SLOPE
Hwang Sun-wŏn

THE DWARF
Cho Se-hŭi

THE RED ROOM: STORIES OF TRAUMA IN CONTEMPORARY KOREA
Bruce and Ju-Chan Fulton, translators

I MET LOH KIWAN
Cho Haejin

Cho Haejin

I MET LOH KIWAN

Translated by Ji-Eun Lee

University of Hawai'i Press

Honolulu

This book is published with the support of the
Literature Translation Institute of Korea (LTI Korea).

Printed in the United States of America
24 23 22 21 20 19 6 5 4 3 2 1

Library of Congress Cataloging-in-Publication Data
Names: Cho, Hae-jin, author. | Lee, Ji-Eun (Korean studies scholar), translator.
Title: I met Loh Kiwan / Haejin Cho ; translated by Ji-Eun Lee.
Other titles: Lo Ki-wan ŭl mannatta. English
Description: Honolulu : University of Hawai'i Press, [2019]
Identifiers: LCCN 2018061663 | ISBN 9780824880026 (cloth : alk. paper) | ISBN 9780824880033 (pbk. : alk. paper)
Subjects: LCSH: Political refugees—Korea (North)—Fiction. | Koreans—Belgium—Fiction.
Classification: LCC PL994.17.H34 L613 2019 | DDC 895.73/5—dc23
LC record available at https://lccn.loc.gov/2018061663

University of Hawai'i Press books are printed on acid-free paper and meet the guidelines for permanence and durability of the Council on Library Resources.

Cover image: funkyfrogstock/shutterstock.com

Contents

Acknowledgments

I met Cho Haejin in the late summer of 2013, when she came to Washington University in St. Louis through the Literature Translation Institute of Korea's Overseas Residence Program. I had just finished reading *I Met Loh Kiwan*, whose arduous quest to find the true meaning of compassion left a deep impression on me. The author arrived in St. Louis with news that this novel had just won the prestigious Sin Dong-yup Prize for Literature. I could not have imagined then that I would be granted the honor of translating this work into English.

For the result you now hold, I must first and foremost thank the author, Cho Haejin, for gifting her beautiful, heartbreaking work to the world. I appreciate her patience over the years while my translation progressed through the inevitable stages to completion.

Bruce Fulton, my mentor, dear friend, and editor of the Modern Korean Fiction Series at the University of Hawai'i Press, read every word of this translation and made major improvements throughout. Without the combined effort of Bruce and his wife, Ju-Chan Fulton, the Korean literature field would not have flourished outside Korea as it does today.

I have been blessed to work again with Pam Kelley on this translation. With her trademark calm and efficiency, Pam has guided me through the labyrinth of publication stages to completion, and words cannot express how grateful I am for her support and her capacity to dissolve pressure and anxiety. I owe similar gratitude to Wendy Lawrence, copy editor for this project, who not only helped perfect the text but also made its final steps engaging, illuminating, and pleasant. I also extend heartfelt gratitude to the staff at University of Hawai'i Press more broadly for their seamless efficiency in producing a polished final product. One quickly learns that this is a blessing, not a right or even an expectation.

I carried this, my first attempt at translating a novel, from St. Louis to Victoria, to Boston, to Brussels, and back to St. Louis. With me most of the way was Tim, my partner in life, and other family members who journeyed with us. I will always remember quiet afternoons in our rented studio apartment in Victoria, BC, where my mother was reading the Korean novel at the dinner table, and my dog Willow was stretched across the floor at her feet, napping, while I hunted for the right word. Such collective moments, where I could break off and free associate about the novel, translation as art, or life generally, were indispensable to this translation, and I am grateful for them all.

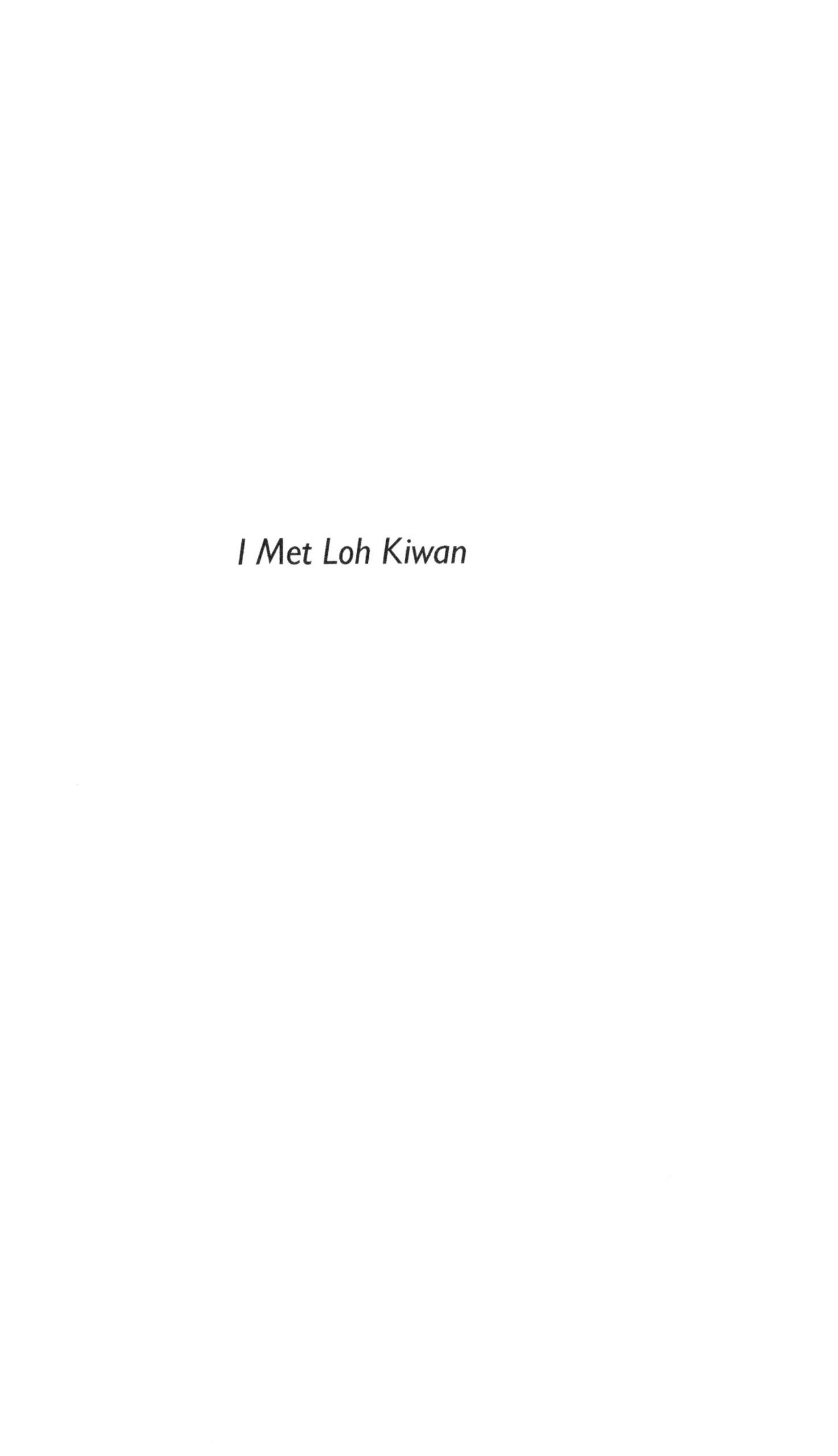

I Met Loh Kiwan

December 7, 2010. Tuesday

In the beginning he was just an initial, L.

He was often called a refugee, a person without a country, lacking identification, an illegal alien who floated from place to place with no legal process to guide him. He was a ghost who could barely communicate with anyone, a stranger from elsewhere who in each new place enjoyed no guarantees of survival or belonging.

With my finger I trace my location on a map of Brussels.

"Gare du Nord."

Reading the map, I recall that in French, *nord* means north, and *gare* means station. Long ago I taught myself French for a year for the sole purpose of reading Marguerite Duras in the original.

I wedge the folded map in my armpit, jam my hands deep in my pockets, and amble toward the Euroline bus depot. A chilly wind blowing through Gare du Nord musses my hair. "Belgium, Brussels," I whisper to myself as I approach the slanted station sign with the bus icon.

At 6 a.m. on Tuesday, December 4, 2007, L. exited a white Euroline bus that arrived here. It had departed Berlin the night before, run close to ten hours, listlessly spat him off at this spot, and continued on to Paris. While everyone else on board slept in bended and folded positions, inanimate as luggage in this bus driving all night through dawn, L. remained wide awake. The dark scenery outside the window was like the same film playing over and over, and it gave no hint of where the bus was heading. He felt like it traversed an orbit somewhere beyond this world: occasional streetlights passed, desolate as stars on their own arc; road signs written in foreign letters flashed like warnings to keep away. Riding the Euroline bus for the first time, he found himself wondering if he was really still alive.

He'd chosen the bus because the broker who bought him the ticket had told him that buses have more lenient passport checks than trains. I try to imagine his appearance: He carries a big cloth bag and wears a shabby pair of jeans, a heavy parka, and a faded brown hat. The crystal of his wristwatch is cracked, his gloves have pills, his scarf, wound several times around his neck, is a drab color, and his sneakers are tattered and dirty. He gets off the bus, and his keen eyes shine with apprehension and bewilderment with each bump from a passerby. His family name is Loh, first name Kiwan. He was then twenty years old, short in stature at five feet two inches and gaunt at just over one hundred pounds. This person had to leave a poor and faraway land on his own without knowing French or Flemish—Belgium's two official languages—or English. "Bel-gium, Bru-ssels, Bel-gium, Bru-ssels," he cycled softly through the names, which remained unfamiliar no matter how many times he heard them. Thus did Loh Kiwan, the stranger without a country, plod south.

~

The clues that substantiate our lives and identities are more tenuous than we imagine, if indeed they exist at all. Unplanned social relations, communities based in customs, and bonds forged of simple attraction, nationality, or kinship are intangible but set limits that demarcate our lives. They might offer consolation that we're not alone, but that consolation is neither permanent nor true. Business cards with a company name and phone number, public documents that record birth, death, marriage, and medical history—what do these prove? A celebratory photograph in a wallet, a journal detailing weekly engagements and routines, passport pages stamped by customs and immigration inside some foreign airport, a rusted key to somewhere, or a dog-eared page in a book may all testify to a life but do not encapsulate it. Even the circadian rhythms of a body accustomed to 7 a.m. rise and 6 p.m. fatigue cannot promise a sense of belonging.

We thus live moment to moment, caught in limbo like a bird with wet wings perched on a branch, unable to take flight, at risk of falling to earth.

Like L.

It was a sentence from L. that led me to Brussels—*the* sentence in his interview with the weekly magazine *H*, a candid confession to the interviewer—that forced me to leave the world I had known.

Reading news magazines and collecting articles of interest was an extension of my work. Thinking I might use some of them for my show, I would stop by a bookstore every Monday to pick up the latest issues and flip through them late into the night. I had returned home from the bookstore that day, too, and was at the dining table browsing to the comforting drone of a TV in the background. That week's special report in the international section of *H* concerned North Korean refugees floating around like ghosts in Belgium. The article featured two men, but it was L.'s story of his travails two years earlier that stayed with me. Because of that one line. Even after I clipped the article and filed it away, the disconcerting presence of that sentence lingered like a phantom on my fingertips.

Two weeks later I e-mailed the journalist who'd written the article. That same day I told Jae, my producer, sitting next to me in the editing room, that I was quitting my job as a lead writer for the show.

Getting up from the editing machine where he reviewed subtitles and audio mixing, my producer crushed the empty paper cup he was holding. Special effects audio from the editing machine played in the awkward silence. Arms crossed, he leaned against the wall and gazed at me. *Unprofessional,* he could have said. Or, *You made a mistake with Yunju, and now you want to run away.* But he said nothing. And whatever he might have said, I had no words to vindicate myself. I have long admitted that I'm not a professional who can rebound from an incident and focus anew on work as if nothing happened. Still, his brusque treatment was hard to take, considering I'd been his not-quite lover, not-quite colleague the last five years.

Of course, these are all excuses.

The next surgery, this one to remove an actual malignant tumor and not a misdiagnosed neurofibroma, was scheduled for the following month. I didn't have the nerve to hear whatever new diagnosis Yunju would face after the operation. I just couldn't. Jae was right. I was about to run away, the only thing I could do to cope.

"So, what are you going to do now?"

He was speaking in honorifics to distance himself from me. To avoid the sight of him across the room, I watched myself doodle on the table with my finger. He and I had retreated into honorifics a few months earlier following an encounter in the parking lot of Yunju's hospital. We never questioned each other about the shift, merely responded in kind when the other spoke that way—our way to spare each other awkwardness.

I looked up. My thoughts strayed from his tired face to the dim editing room, then to our intimate breaths and voices and how they used to dwell here. In that moment I hated the indiscriminate workings of memory, how it replays things I want to remember alongside things I want to forget. However low the volume is set, sound is integral to the scene being replayed—it's how memory works. Now that I'd no longer see him at work, future reminiscences would have to include not only his face and how it used to make me laugh but also our last moments in this editing room, the uneasiness in the air, and how tensely I listened to the sequence of editing sounds.

He coughed, maybe to break my silent stare.

"I may leave for Brussels." Well, I had to say *something.*

"Brussels, the capital of Belgium?"

"I . . . think there's someone there I ought to see."

It was a cryptic thing to say. He adjusted his glasses and murmured, "Brussels." Not *Why Brussels, of all places?* The single word, spoken half to himself, deprived me of the response I'd prepared after deciding to resign: I've been thinking of writing from a stranger's point of view about someone who was forced to become a stranger there. Not for a future broadcast but maybe as a novel.

L.

Head lowered, I silently called his name. L., who had been living like a ghost in a faraway land, became for me an entry code to a new world.

After a long silence, he said we should meet one last time before I left. Gloomily, I watched his lips curl up as if to force a smile, then harden that way like an actor halted just before he was supposed to laugh out loud. I smiled back much the same way. And there we were, grinning vacantly, forcing ourselves for a bit too long. I could hardly believe time still flowed at such a moment. I then explained that this would be my final week, adding that a month's material was already in hand and that scriptwriters are easy to come by. I proceeded to ask for that week's salary as my last paycheck, saying I saw no reason to remain any longer. He gazed stiffly at me for a moment. It was an exacting gaze, the sort that could yield the precise digital measure of an object's size and weight and then produce exact replicas.

"Producer Ryu!"

In came one of the assistant directors to hand him a document, apparently something requiring immediate approval. I rose and with a nod to Jae and then the assistant, walked toward the door. I guess it was when my hand closed over the doorknob that I heard Jae's voice suggesting the two of us and Yunju meet for a farewell dinner. I nodded insincerely without turning back. "Perhaps not." My honest answer came only after the door shut behind me. I can't explain why neither of us had conceded our feelings for each other even at that moment, which was essentially a breakup. I gazed down at my fingertips, where L.'s words had lingered earlier, but saw nothing. That absence became resolve: the first thing I did after returning home that night was e-mail the journalist who had interviewed L.

Three days later came his cordial reply. He introduced himself as an occasional contributor to *H*—he wasn't one of their staff reporters—who lived abroad and wrote on current issues in his host country. He'd fallen out of touch with L. after the interview but could introduce me to a Korean who knew much more about him. I sent a reply with repeated thank-yous, and the next moment I purchased a flight to Brussels leaving Incheon Airport in ten days' time. Three months had passed since the discovery that Yunju's tumors had turned malignant and the start of radiation treatment and chemotherapy.

An elderly man in a black suit is playing a violin as I exit Gare du Nord. His pants are stained with mud, and his shirt is heavily wrinkled, but his tie is clean and neat. Gray hair that reminds me of Beethoven's sways beautifully in the winter breeze. He is playing "Vocalise" by Rachmaninoff, a familiar piece from trips in Jae's car. I take a two-euro coin from my purse and drop it into the open violin case in front of his old shoes. Without stopping, the man gives me a warm wink.

Loh, too, heard a violin here three years ago. Hearing the piece for the first time, he didn't know its name, and he couldn't have asked because he didn't speak the language, so we can't know for sure if this same musician played "Vocalise" on this street back then. The unknown melody would have provided momentary consolation for the twenty-year-old who knew nothing about the unsettling new world he faced. Enthralled by the music, he set his suitcase down, took a fifty-cent piece from an inner pocket of his jacket, and dropped it into the violin case. It was one of the coins the Korean-Chinese broker who'd bought him a Euroline bus ticket to Brussels at the airport in Berlin had handed to him.

Later, walking through downtown Brussels, Loh occasionally encountered street musicians playing violins, accordions, or guitars. In his diary he described seeing in them his own future of begging and quietly turning away, suppressing an urge to leave each a coin. Not much money remained after he'd paid the broker's expenses, including the plane ticket. What had started as 650 euros was his inheritance from his mother. The money *was* his mother. Later he wrote that among the many tunes he'd heard on the street, the most beautiful came from a young guitarist who sat in front of a subway station with a big dog. Never had he missed his mother and his home village as he did then. He learned later at Foyer Selah that the tune was "Knocking on Heaven's Door." Foyer Selah, which means something like "pleasant resting space," accommodated refugees in limbo between a temporary residence permit and the finalization of refugee status. It was there at 9 a.m., when Sylvie arrived at her office and turned on the radio, that Loh again heard the beautiful, haunting melody. He'd been mopping the second-floor hallway, froze in place, and then walked spellbound, mop in hand, toward the music's source. He stopped at the stairs leading down to the office. Might he have succumbed to an uncontrollable surge of remorse, sniffling like a little child? Sylvie would have risen from her paper-strewn desk by the window and found Loh in this state. She could have guessed what haunted his eyes, now fixed on the radio. Sylvie, the compassionate Belgian, wrote the name of the song and the artist on a yellow Post-it note. The note is attached to the diary entry from March 25, 2008. After adding the note to the diary page, Loh had looked up the words "knock," "heaven," and "door" in his English-Korean dictionary and eventually understood the meaning of the title. Knocking on heaven's door. That night, lying on his bed and staring up at the ceiling, Loh would have repeated the name of the song many times.

I close his diary at the scene where Loh hears the violin playing at Gare du Nord. The violinist has finished "Vocalise" and is now playing "Ave Maria." I proceed along the pedestrian walkway toward the subway station. The initial plan was to walk to Grand-Place, the central plaza, but maybe due to the time difference, what should have been a short walk takes over an hour, and I am weighed down by fatigue.

To enter Pak's apartment near the Leopold train station, one needs two different keys for two different doors. The first door is the main entrance to the apartment building; the other indicates apartment 605, at the far end of the hallway from the elevator. Beyond these two doors is a space where I can indulge myself. Two keys promise a sealed space that shields my identity from this strange city of Brussels.

Having stopped at a market on my way from Gare du Nord, I stumble into Pak's apartment with a paper bag of groceries. You might think I've lived in this apartment for a while, given how I change into slippers and head straight to the bathroom to wash my hands. My toothbrush resides in the plastic cup on the vanity, and the two towels I brought from Korea, one blue, the other white, hang from the towel rack. My toiletries, in a vinyl pack, occupy the shower stall, whose blue console holds shampoo, conditioner, and hair essence in a neat row. Other things of mine are likewise finding their natural places in the three bedrooms, the living room, and the kitchen.

Unexpectedly, I am using this luxury apartment in Brussels for free.

The contributor to *H* who lives in Brussels took my call eagerly and arranged for us to meet the next day at a Korean restaurant. There, he would introduce me to Pak, the contact he'd mentioned in his e-mail who knew L.

Probably in his late sixties, Pak gave the impression of a stubborn old man who had retained his dignity and self-respect. For a long time, his face remained free of sorrow or pointless emotional exertion, and his eyes, peering beyond thick, dark-rimmed glasses, seemed lonely. He told me that the North Korean refugee had, regrettably, left Brussels a year ago and was now in London. "Regrettably," he said, but his voice carried no hint of regret. I said it was fine. I didn't know how to address Pak, so my reply lacked a title for him. The journalist called him "Doctor," but this formula seemed unbefitting.

"Seeing as how you're a writer, may I call you Kim *chakka?*"

Pak must have been thinking about titles also, as this was his first question when the food arrived. I nodded, raising chopsticks to my mouth. Kim *chakka.* Kim the writer. I was all too familiar with the title, one I'd long used socially. Yunju had called me that in the beginning. I liked her voice when she said it. Yunju was a kid with a grown-up voice that convinced you she understood whatever confusion and anxiety you had. When Yunju called me Kim *chakka* while we were having coffee, listening to music, or going for a walk, I was never lonely. But my heart would grow heavy questioning how a meager seventeen years had cultivated such a voice. Did the bulge spreading from her right cheek to her chin, which drew people's eyes wherever she went, rob her of the right to feel beautiful and proud? Did it instead give her a voice that could console others in their loneliness? The thought of so wretched and cruel a gift caused rage to well up inside me. The bulge was Yunju's candid life of facing away from people; it was made not of muscles, blood vessels, and nerves but of rash gazes and the scars they leave on a young heart, of tears falling unseen.

"You can call me Unni," I told her one day, and finally she smiled like a seventeen-year-old and said, "Are you sure, Unni?" Unni. Big sis.

"You can call me Pak when we're alone," said Pak when the journalist left for the restroom. I replied that I couldn't but thought it suited him better than "Doctor" or "Sir," for it indicated no hierarchy.

Over tea in place of dessert, I learned much about Pak. He was born in Pyongyang, went to a "people's school"—like elementary school in the South—crossed the border with his mother during the Korean War, and lived in Seoul. As mothers are wont to do, Pak's mother supported him through all kinds of troubles, darkened always by the shadow of poverty. Pak was a medical student in Seoul when he got involved in a political controversy and left to study in France with his wife, whom he'd met while attending university. He could not bring his mother with them. While Pak continued his medical studies at a university in France, his wife faithfully supported him by working odd jobs in restaurants and grocery stores. After obtaining his certificate, he practiced as a surgeon in a small hospital outside Paris. In his late forties, he moved to Brussels and opened a clinic with a Belgian doctor. This led smoothly to Belgian citizenship and a stable life of financial means. Two children followed: they got educated, landed jobs, got married, and left for other cities. His mother and wife eventually passed due to illness, one in Korea and the other in Brussels. Listening to this concise inventory of a person's life, I pondered the fragility of every human being. From the moment he emerges between his mother's bloodied thighs until death finds him, a person is utterly alone, and that fateful loneliness infused Pak's short narrative.

Pak added that he had stopped practicing five years earlier, after his wife's death. He smiled—the only time—as he told me he'd been volunteering with the Korean community in Belgium, unable to tolerate the amount of free time he suddenly possessed. The smile was bitter and desolate, not bright. One of his new tasks was to help obtain refugee status for someone like Loh by determining his nationality. Pak had proved invaluable: only a person like him, fluent in both Korean and French and whose knowledge of North Korea derived from being a Pyongyang native, could perform such a task. With European countries recognizing North Korean nationals as political exiles and granting them refugee status, many Chinese impostors tried to pass among the applicants. These impostors included Korean ethnics who spoke Korean with an accent similar to that of true North Korean defectors, and Pak was indispensable in filtering out these fakes while recognizing the real thing.

After we left the restaurant, the journalist returned home, and I walked with Pak through the rainy streets of Brussels. Our shoulders bumped as we shared Pak's large umbrella while strolling near the Palais Royal, where the Belgian royal family resides. I heard quite a lot about Loh Kiwan from him, but because Loh was now in London, I could not meet him anytime soon. When the rain became a downpour, we retreated to a small pub. Pak ordered a stout, and I chose a red-tinted beer that had cherries. Out of the blue, Pak asked why I'd become interested in North Korean defectors. *Finally!*—I'd expected the question much sooner. I told him about Loh's short statement in the magazine. I wanted to add that his words had awakened in me a desire to write something other than television scripts and that I wanted this new writing to be good, but for some reason these words didn't come out. Perhaps I foresaw no answer if Pak then asked why Loh's sentence had planted such a desire to write. But Pak only peered at me from across the table. Occasionally, his gaze sharpened as if he'd detected something hidden in me, but it didn't faze me. I gradually became comfortable with the calm silence that settled over us. It was like a soothing light: not too bright, not so dark as to create fear, reassuringly calm.

After we left the pub, Pak took me to the apartment.

He told me that after he'd retired, he had moved to the suburbs but kept the apartment where he and his wife had lived and used it as an office. His age made it difficult to commute, though, and it soon became obvious he was wasting his time since he had nothing in particular to research. And so he suggested I use the apartment during my stay in Brussels. I was grateful but, unused to such kindness from someone I'd just met, I wavered, thinking I should at least have the means to repay him. Noticing my hesitation, he said in his usual casual tone that I could write a good work in return. The next thing I knew, he was giving me Loh Kiwan's diary, mailed to him before Loh had left for England, and a copy of the personal statement he'd written at the office that evaluates refugee status applications. Those documents, keys to a life I'd first happened across in a one-line sentence in a magazine, proved that the opaque stranger I'd known as L. was indeed a person, the formidable existence of Loh Kiwan. I placed the diary and personal statement in my handbag.

"After the operation you'll be pain-free. You won't have to suffer anymore."

"I don't have to live *that* boring a life, Unni."

"Being unaware of certain things isn't bad, is it?"

"So you want to be someone with no regrets, Unni? How would you write anything then?"

"Does regret make you a better writer?"

"You won't only write for shows your whole life, will you?"

"You think I have something else in mind?"

"Yes."

"Like what?"

"Like . . . a novel."

I recalled this short conversation with Yunju in the hospital lobby.

After a shower I power up my laptop on the desk, open the music files, and hit Play. In the kitchen I take bottled water, low-fat milk, carrots, onions, oranges, apples, ham, cheese, bread, eggs, and a small pack of beef from the shopping bag and place them in the refrigerator. It occurs to me: Why is this so easy and convenient? I take walks, shop for groceries at the market, and in the evenings listen to music while making supper. I settle on the sofa and lose myself in books I brought from Korea, sometimes indulging in a late morning that lasts until noon. Some days I urge the phone to ring, others I pray it won't. No calls yet with news of Yunju or Jae.

Leaving the other groceries on the dining table, I move to the living-room sofa, which I've been using as my bed. I can borrow a living space, but sleeping in a bed once shared by Pak and his wife seems inappropriate, so I've kept to the sofa since my arrival. As I settle myself there, a bout of coughing erupts. Finally suppressing it, I get up, open my suitcase, and take out the medicine kit. I have felt since the morning that I was coming down with something. In the kit are aspirin, allergy pills, sleeping pills, and digestive aids. Like a child with a hand in the cookie jar, I close my eyes, reach in, fumble about, grab a pill, and wash it down with water. Only then do I note the packaging: a sleeping pill. Good thing. I want to sleep anyway. Back to the sofa I go.

I have yet to convince myself that I'm entitled to write about Loh Kiwan.

A nightmare awakens me. That scene from three months ago. The one-liner that led me here and the nightmare are closely intertwined despite the time and space separating the two. Unable to raise myself from the sofa, I stare at the dark ceiling.

"It's turned malignant. I'm sorry."

The voice of Yunju's doctor echoes through the scene in the dream, and I feel a sudden chill. I look for my alarm watch as I hoist myself up, motivated by the prospect of a hot shower. But the watch is not in its usual place, to the left of the headboard. Then it kicks in: I'm in Brussels, not Seoul. What led me here? How did I come this far? I look around. Perhaps there's a hidden pathway to the single bed in my studio apartment in Mapo, Seoul.

Sleep eludes me. I flip open the phone I'd tucked beneath the sofa. It's 2 a.m. The five-hundred-milligram chemical concoction put me to sleep for less than five fitful hours.

I take a hot shower. Then I towel myself dry, put on clean underwear, spread body lotion all over and work it in, put on pajamas, trim my nails, gently clean out my ears with cotton swabs, and brush and blow-dry my hair. *I hate you.* If a total stranger had blurted out something like that in the wee hours, I would not have been too startled. I turn the blow-dryer off and look around anxiously. "Shall we get married?" The audible reminiscence echoes about the desolate living room. It is Jae's voice, flying to me from the faraway hallway outside Yunju's hospital room, number 1027. I'm embarrassed at how Jae's proposal still allows me to console myself. At this moment, it's the only thing that embarrasses me.

That day, like others, I was hovering outside Yunju's hospital room, unable to make myself enter or leave; I could only look down at my shoes. Jae spoke quietly from behind me. He chose the wrong day. But every day was the wrong day since we'd heard Yunju's tumor had turned malignant. I didn't respond to Jae, who had followed me silently from where we worked. He waited at a distance as he proposed to me, in a tone one might use to suggest grabbing a bite to eat. An uncomfortable silence is more miserable than an outright rejection, but I ignored Jae's discomfort. He must have spoken on the spur of the moment, and his regret was obvious. We'd never confessed love for each other, so the word "marriage" didn't carry much weight. We avoided each other's gaze, proceeded to the basement parking lot, and hurried our separate ways without a good-bye. I unlocked the door to my car, then turned and walked toward Jae's. Already in the driver's seat, he noticed me approaching, rolled down the window, and stuck his head out. Gazing down at his stunned face, I asked him to treat me as a coworker and leave it at that. I said it without emotion, like someone who had long been preparing for such an occasion. I didn't explain myself, but Jae should have known. I cannot be happy—I cannot allow myself that. My soul cried out behind this mask that feigned detachment. As I'd expected, Jae simply nodded and did not ask the reason. Whatever his emotions then, I failed to read them in his face.

Jae's car started a minute or two later.

Only after his car exited the parking garage did I begin to wonder. What would my first reminiscence of him be? Jae immersed in a script? Jae on location and constantly in motion, checking the camera angles and subjects? Jae's deep voice speaking after filming to the person featured in that week's show? Or the disillusioned expression I used to see in his face as our program ended, and the credits rolled by?

I want to convince myself through these reminiscences that Jae and I had become estranged enough to require formal honorific speech with each other. But more than that, I need assurance that I had also let go of perhaps the greatest happiness in my life, that I had suffered as much as I could, and that Jae and I had been fated to separate. For the moment, I decide to ignore the futility of this attempt at consolation, which amounted to no more than a rationalization.

December 9, 2010. Thursday

Good Sleep Hostel, 32 Rue du Damier, is located behind the Galeria Inno, a prominent department store in Brussels' busiest shopping district, Rue Neuve. Christmas is two weeks away, and Rue Neuve is decorated with magnificent trees and brilliant colors, like a holiday-themed park. As I turn onto Rue du Damier, I realize what a landmark Galeria Inno is, especially next to this dark, drab alley that's right out of a gangster movie. Not a Christmas tree in sight. An oil drum firepit would be at home here.

After dropping a coin in the violin case, Loh walked aimlessly along the boulevard. A hotel, a bank, intersections, crosswalks, a woman eating a bun, a man smoking and walking, people in neon vests picking up garbage . . . While he looked for a place to spend the night, his brain must have been busy storing these images so he wouldn't get lost. His hand clutched a map of Brussels acquired at the Gare du Nord Visitor Information kiosk, but he didn't know how to read it. For a week before leaving Yanji in China, the broker had given them tips, including getting a map wherever they went.

He also taught them brief, strict directives, as if from a spy's field manual. These stuck fast in Loh's mind: Find a hostel rather than a hotel. Take a single room even if it cost more. Go to the South Korean embassy as soon as possible and ask for help.

Without a grasp of the language, Loh must have memorized simple phrases by sound alone: "Wud-u-let-mi-now-chiip-gud-hostel?" But a foreign language is like a code one needs in order to enter that world. What puzzles me now is how Loh managed to find Good Sleep Hostel, located in a back alley, without knowing the city's code.

Showing my passport to a gum-chewing woman in a t-shirt and jeans, probably in her twenties, I ask for a single room. Her expression conveys how upset she is about wasting the most brilliant days of her life at a reception desk. No doubt her mundane life away from this desk is equally boring and predictable and just as imaginative as the name of this hostel. Loh, knowing neither of the two official languages of this country, or English, might have broken into a cold sweat in front of this strict and humorless woman.

"We don't have a single room," the woman says without emotion.

There were no single rooms three years ago, either. Loh must have stared blankly at this woman already annoyed by a guest who spoke no English. She might have made an *X* with two arms and gesticulated impatiently, Loh only then understanding what her antisocial code aimed to communicate. Or maybe this sour woman was not even here three years ago.

"I'd like a double room, then, but I'll use it by myself, please."

Loh couldn't have uttered this sentence in English like I did—he'd have used both hands to express himself. In my mind he raises a finger on the right hand to say single room, shows two fingers on the left hand and makes an *X* like the woman did, and repeats the sequence several times—a comedian in a silent film, or an incompetent and clumsy supporting actor who receives jeers instead of laughter. Imagining his actions makes me a little sad.

"Okay. Forty euros please," the woman says, pushing pen and registration form at me.

Forty euros was big money for Loh. With his fund of 650 euros, he wouldn't be able to stay longer than two weeks even if he ate just once a day. He promised himself he would reach the South Korean embassy—his last hope, the destination on which all further dreams depended—within a week. Loh turned aside to remove a waterproof pouch from an inner pocket and counted out forty euros. I stop writing as a dull pain, spawned by the image, ascends to my heart. One of the few times I had stopped reading Loh's diary was toward the end, when I learned the significance of the money he carried. The sentence from the magazine that led me here described the same moment.

"How long have you worked here, by the way—two years, five years?" I ask, as I submit the completed registration.

"This is my fourth year," the woman snaps. "Why do you ask?"

It seems more likely now that Loh obtained his double room from this woman. If so, then her callousness marked his first halting communication with this country.

"I stayed here three years ago, but I don't remember if I saw you then. I stayed in room 308 . . ."

"Yes? I don't remember you either. Lots of people pass through here every day."

"You're right, but . . ."

"But what?"

"May I stay in room 308 if it's available? I want to remind myself of last time."

"Room 308? It's vacant. Would you like it?"

"Yes, thank you."

"I'll give you the key, but you can't use the room until after three o'clock. Just leave your bags there."

"Okay."

She doesn't smile.

There's an elevator, but I use the stairs as Loh did. My black carry-on is almost empty and easy to tote. Like the wristwatch with the cracked face that Loh had worn three years earlier, my cell phone reads 11:30 a.m. Loh had wandered the freezing streets for five and a half hours to find this place and barely managed to get a room.

Finally, I stand before room 308.

I imagine Loh, shoulders hunched, heaving a sigh as he unlocked the door with a crudely shaped key dangling from a plastic bar. Maybe the sigh marked his survival thus far. Or perhaps he stood about to enter this coldest and loneliest room in the city thinking he was absolutely alone and might finally die.

The room's furniture consists of two single beds beneath a window. There is no toilet or bathroom. A microwave oven or television set would have seemed opulent in a room that doesn't even have an electric kettle. A gray sink to the left of the door evinces the heavy gloom of a piece of installation art. I approach the window, lean my carry-on against the wall, and open the curtains and window. The pushout window has a lock that prevents it from opening all the way. A parking garage belonging to Galeria Inno comes into view. No cars have arrived yet, so the structure is lean and bare, desolate as winter. The wind of December blows cold air into room 308 and out again. If the winter wind of Brussels had a shape, it might be a wicked giant.

The first thing Loh did in this room was sink to his knees and bow toward the North, to his mother. I have no sense of which way is north. Instead, I take a lighter and cigarettes from my handbag and light up. It's what he did next. Puffing absently beside the open window, Loh gazed with faraway eyes at the parking tower, toward a different continent where he spoke the language perfectly, whose customs he didn't have to research. Toward his mother, who just by holding his gaze reminded him of why he lived.

Loh's diary says nothing about his hometown. His only mention of it occurs in the personal statement he submitted as part of his refugee status application. "My name is Loh Kiwan, and I was born on May 18, 1987, in Sector 7, Onseong-gun, Seseon-li, North Hamgyeong Province, Democratic People's Republic of Korea." The statement, which starts with this sentence, is about five pages long, half of it describing his home and family. It also notes that Loh's father, who died in a mining accident when Loh was five years old, was born in Sector 3 in the same town and that his mother, his only other immediate family, was born in Sector 5. Her name was Choe Yeong-ae, born November 23, 1965; she died September 11, 2007, at a little-known surgical hospital in Yanji, China. The abbreviated chronicle of her life, scribbled down on several sheets of paper, had passed from one hand to another to arrive finally in mine. I take a deep drag. A momentary thought, that no heart will break if I disappear quietly from this world, dissolves in the smoke.

"Hey!"

A high-pitched voice from behind me. I turn slowly and there stands the same dark-skinned woman whom Loh encountered with confusion three years ago. She looks like early forties, wears blue work clothes, and has a vacuum cleaner at her side. Three years ago she unlocked the door with her set of keys, saw Loh, and banged on the wall.

"No smoking here! And this is housecleaning time. Get out now and come back after check-in, or I'll call the police!"

She would have yelled at Loh like this three years ago.

The only word Loh would have recognized in her outburst was "police," one of the words taught during prep time in Yanji. It would have left Loh frozen with fear. The woman had only mentioned police because of his cigarette, not his illegal status, but until he realized that, Loh could only cling to the window like a prisoner awaiting the executioner's bullet. He would not have registered ash from the still-burning cigarette falling onto his foot.

I stub out the cigarette on the windowsill, leaving the luggage but taking my handbag as I leave. I make a point to glare at the woman standing by the door with her arms crossed. *Hey, this is my room. Don't you think it's a bit much, mentioning the police because I'm smoking in a room I already paid for?* I hope my eyes convey this message, but the cleaning lady's hard gaze and raised head project a clear resolve to dismiss any objection. I slam the door behind me. The diminutive Asian man, who still looked for his first chance to say "hello" or "bonjour," softly closed the door and realized that his life in this city would be full of disregard, contempt, overblown wariness, and unnecessary misunderstandings.

~

"I feel like I'm on a different planet," his diary continues.

As Loh left the hostel and walked down Rue Neuve, he thought this was a different world. In the morning, before he'd found a place to stay, most shops hadn't opened yet, and few shoppers were about. His urgency to find lodging had blinded him to the splendor around him. Only after Loh found a hostel room and went back out onto the street did he grasp how little the place where he now stood resembled the world he knew, and for a while his fear dissolved in fascination. Glittering display cases with pricey merchandise, up-tempo music blaring in his ears, customers greeted by beautiful women in short-sleeved shirts and short skirts despite the midwinter season, their language ringing like a song, tall descendants of giants striding down the street with shopping bags in hand and satisfaction on their faces . . .

Loh had tasted capitalism in Yanji, but Yanji was no Brussels. The shapes and sizes of people walking the streets were different, as was the language, and the mood of the two cities had little in common. Capitalism in Yanji felt like a fragile structure slapped together in haste, whereas the edifice of Brussels was a sturdy framework for genuine affluence and freedom. Yanji strove anxiously to create and fill its needs. Brussels was already full, arrogant, and exclusive.

Loh frowned as images flashed to mind: Malnourished kids who had stopped growing. Young people with their hair falling out. Young laborers bartering machine parts from their factory—their lifeline—for cheap grain from China. People who, even at the moment of arrest for stealing food from their collaborative farm storage, reached desperately for one more handful to eat. News of deaths every other day. Hospitals without basic medicinal supplies. Office buildings without heat or air-conditioning and supplied only occasionally with electricity. Schools that could no longer afford textbooks or supplies for students. Was it all a mirage? Loh couldn't believe that on the opposite side of this affluent world there existed just such a community, an entire nation desperately poor and blighted by famine. More impossible still, he himself came from that world. The moment he thought of his home, he felt shame, like a stranger who had showed up uninvited at an exclusive party in some faraway land.

Loh continues writing: "The people in this country are like the descendants of Titans, and their language sounds like glass marbles rolling in their mouths." A language that sounds so tender it could be used for whispering sweet words, a language that doesn't sound capable of carrying shouts, screams, or cries of nature. How, then, did Loh look to the people of Brussels, a place where starvation is only an indirect reference in history books or films, where risking one's life crossing borders is virtual reality in a computer game? The pathological anxiety of a person who has lost his country was as unimaginable to the people here as it is to me.

"A little farther," I whisper to myself as I walk.

Which store was it?

Loh stopped to peer into a shop window displaying a slender mannequin clothed in a black wool coat. A little plaque at its feet showed a price of 2,320 euros. It was an imaginary, surreal number for Loh. Besides, the only family he could imagine buying the coat for had departed.

All winter long Mother went to work at bathhouses and karaoke bars, wearing an army surplus pullover with barely any padding left. Winter was colder in Yanji than in Brussels. During the day she cleaned the bathhouse; in the evenings she worked the taverns and sang for drunken customers at the bar. Loh wanted her to stop these evening jobs, but he didn't prevent her from leaving each day. Life in Yanji was dangerous for a young man without positive identification. Young men are easily noticed by the Chinese police, and once caught they have no guarantees. Loh occasionally inquired at illegal logging operations or construction sites but was rejected every time for his short stature and lack of strength, traits that had marked him since childhood. Every time he would turn away disheartened. From a small dark room provided by a maternal relative, he would watch his mother hurrying from one job to the next, before leafing half-heartedly through books he'd brought from home and Chinese-language textbooks donated by a Korean church. Loh spent his nineteenth and twentieth years waiting for an elusive chance to work, hating his diminutive body and always-alert mind.

The McDonald's, located on 24 Rue Neuve. Is this the one a starving Loh walked into?

There was a McDonald's in Yanji. He'd reached Yanji after a midnight river crossing, a wait in the woods for first light, and a fifteen-hour walk into furious headwinds. After finding his mother's relative, he finally caught a bus into the city. His first encounter with capitalism consisted of McDonald's and KFC on billboards, Motorola cell phones in people's hands, and cars with Toyota and Mercedes logos populating the streets—capitalist codes that promised grandeur. During his years in Yanji, however, Loh hadn't once indulged in a hamburger from McDonald's, located in the heart of downtown. Motorola cell phones and Toyotas were even further removed from his experience. Loh rarely got the chance to step out of the poor and remote town where he lived, a thirty-plus-minute bus ride from downtown Yanji; most of the time, he remained in near confinement in a dark room that blended day and night.

After a long hesitation, Loh entered the Rue Neuve McDonald's. A bell at the door rang, welcoming people with money to spend. As it would have been three years ago, McDonald's is full of people—no vacant seats. I stand in a long line waiting my turn to order. The only fast food Loh knew at the time were hamburgers and Coke; he knew of no other options and could not ask what else was available. The line is getting shorter. Loh would have gotten nervous again.

In his diary Loh did not record the name of that first hamburger. He just called it a huge beef-tasting burger. He hadn't eaten for a day, not since the in-flight meal to Berlin. With a shiver Loh felt the sweet, hot meat surround his tongue as he finished the burger in eager bites and gulped at a Coke that stung the inside of his mouth. Capitalism was delicious. As long as one had cash, capitalism seemed to promise every necessity; it even nurtured an unfounded optimism when you filled your belly. After the meal Loh felt relief for the first time since arriving in Brussels—no, for the first time since leaving home.

I grab a vacated seat by the window and look out on the streets, as Loh had. A Big Mac meal sits in front of me. Through the window I see a woman in a black cape holding an infant, shivering in the cold as she begs for coins. She's one of many Gypsies in Europe. I read in a guidebook that Gypsies often beg with a baby in arms to help generate compassion. But most people walking the streets of Brussels seem immune to such tactics and seldom drop coins in the woman's paper cup. I return my gaze to the interior of McDonald's. Eating, swallowing, drinking lips shine with grease as the patrons laugh and talk through their meals. I sit among them. Even in this mundane pocket of Brussels, the haves and have-nots occupy two very different worlds.

Since when, though, do I belong to this indoor space.

I have no appetite, but not because of the Gypsy woman or the greasy lips. Maybe it's because Yunju's story is creeping like evening gloom into this disinterested and sadly bifurcated world. Yunju once told me she often gulped cold rice after her mother replaced her dad as the family breadwinner. This was during an unexpected day off when special programming had caused a last-minute schedule change, so, pizza in hand, I visited Yunju's place in Imun-dong, where she lived alone. The test results were in, and the operation would take place two weeks later. I probably wanted to treat Yunju to a meal, such as pizza, that wasn't so nutritious but would be missed once she faced dietary restrictions.

It had all started, she told me, when she was about nine years old, and her little sister was eager to start elementary school. It was an age when practically anything would help you grow. Yunju's father had worked in construction until a pile of bricks fell on him and injured his back. No longer mobile, he couldn't even reach the kitchen to help prepare food for the girls and instead lapsed into self-deprecating monologues as he struggled with the prospect of becoming useless. For two long years, he battled against the huge shapeless monster of his circumstances. Yunju's mother, who'd started working at a nearby factory packing plastic kitchen containers, rarely came home in time for supper. When the dinner hour arrived, Yunju would leave the house to avoid the sight of an empty table and the sound of her father's muttering. Time crawled while she waited for her mother.

"But you know what?" asked Yunju, grabbing a slice of pizza. "Mom brought pizza home one day. It had gone cold, but I remember thinking there can't be anything yummier than this. My sister and I had a race to see who could eat faster. I won and she started bawling. Dad was lying down facing the wall and wouldn't turn around when mom offered him a bite. Mom looked at my sister and me, didn't say a word, and you should have seen how hollow her eyes were. And of course in the wee hours of the morning, I paid for gorging myself like that. It was my turn to bawl as I crouched over the toilet throwing everything up. And that was . . . the last."

"The last what?" I asked, heedless of the answer I was forcing.

"Mom left early the next morning. For good. That's when Dad really went crazy. And I think that's when my right cheek started swelling up."

After she finished her story, we continued to smile at each other and share the pizza, but I found myself unable to meet her eyes whenever difficulty in swallowing darkened her face. The food sat heavy in my stomach, and after I'd cleaned the table and was getting ready to leave, I was hit with nausea. Yunju massaged my back for a long while, then tried a home remedy in which she bled the tips of my thumbs with needles.

I push aside the burger and Coke and flip open my cell phone. Making sure I haven't used up my roaming service, I punch in the number for Yunju's hospital room and try to think of what I'll say first. *I'm in Brussels. The capital of Belgium, like I told you. How's the chemo going? Your operation is coming up. How are you feeling? You're not going to die on me, right?* No, these anxious words ring hollow; I did run from her, after all. I could say, *I came here wanting to find out more about someone but instead of meeting him in person, I'm kind of following his footsteps. Do you think I'm being a coward? Am I doing the right thing?*

I shake my head. I don't like any of this.

Maybe I can be a bit more honest since I'm not seeing her face to face? I could tell her I'm finding familiar scenes in a stranger's life, someone who used to be only L., an initial. It's ringing. I imagine Yunju merely looking on as the phone clamors for attention. After ten or twelve rings, the connection turns to static, as if someone is about to answer, and I quickly close my phone. Maybe I didn't want to talk to her in the first place. Yunju seldom answers the landline in her room. That's why I called it instead of her cell.

The current time floats up in the phone's tiny window—3 p.m. Time to return to Good Sleep Hostel and fetch my luggage.

What is the nature of pity? What is it made of, and how does it grow and then diminish? For it to be sincere, what aspect of experience must it recognize, and what must it reject?

Such were my thoughts when I started working on the program Jae was producing. I'd rarely thought seriously about pity before meeting him.

We worked together for five years on this show, a twenty-five-minute minidocumentary with two episodes each on a variety of people in need: a single mother whose son suffered from a rare disease, a girl weighing two hundred kilograms due to an uncontrollable appetite, a laborer who immigrated to Korea chasing a dream and a future before losing both legs in a workplace accident, a senior living alone with a serious illness and unable to afford medical treatment. These and others in society's blind spots let their existence be known through our program, which solicited real-time call-ins from viewers to the Automated Response Service (ARS), an automated number that translated each call into a one-dollar donation.

This was the first program for which I was the lead writer. Previously, I'd spent a year as a junior assistant, then three years as a junior writer. My last work as a junior writer had been for a fifty-minute medical documentary series. We would choose from a pool of submitted stories and then follow the patient for several weeks. It occurred to me during this time that while those with physical illness can recover in a hospital, those with mental illness have nowhere to go. Although I was only a junior writer, the shifting pressures at work meant I sometimes wrote whole episodes on my own. The episode that moved a producer named Ryu Jae concerned a thirty-two-year-old man caring full time for his father, who suffered from dementia and diabetes, while he himself coped with incurable myotonic dystrophy.

At a dinner meeting with the staff and narrators, Jae said he liked the episode's simple narration. That was when he and I first met.

Jae also said my characterization of the patient's pain rang true. Tickled that I'd finally become a lead writer, I nodded enthusiastically, gesturing with a shot glass full of whatever clear spirit Jae had poured me. I couldn't admit that I didn't even know what my truth was. Besides, judging whether one is truthful, assessing why truth remains elusive, and dwelling on the resolve needed to keep generating script even when it isn't truthful—one cannot indulge such graces while keeping a hectic schedule. I would wake up to a day of shooting, write through the night, and then have editing to do before getting any sleep. Meanwhile, accidents happened on-site, personnel on both sides of the camera lens would call at all hours, and producers would wave my script and yell at me to make it more dramatic.

What did it amount to, those four years at the broadcasting company?

I know in a mechanical sense what I did: I produced scripts nonstop; my twenties amounted to the piles of paper no one ever flips through again after an episode airs. Despite the simplicity of the work itself, the multitude of tasks it involved exhausted me. Yet I immersed myself in them to help endure other things. A lazy producer who sat at his desk all day, making writers do all the work of contacting episode personnel and hunting for sites. A lead writer whose hysteria made our phones ring all hours of the night. Bosses who kept me at work until after the last bus had gone, knowing my salary wasn't enough for cab fares. A senior writer who nonchalantly sent me to fetch a feminine hygiene product. Fellow junior writers who scrambled over one another to network when the season came to an end. Someone who stole another's project plan and submitted it as his own. A person who consumed and amplified unverified rumors. Dealing with such people taught me accepted workplace practice. I learned the efficacy of coasting, of pouring passion into baseless malice and jealousy, of shunning responsibility. I learned how sufficient self-interest can compensate for not being truly needed. I also witnessed how a person so lacking ends up depleted, incapable of either smiling or crying.

Having survived so many such programs, sincerity nowhere in sight, I had felt nothing when Jae mentioned truthfulness five years ago. In my numbness, I didn't grasp that his comment was cynical, a recognition that the pain of the person featured would be conveyed for maximum effect, not for fidelity to truth.

The show aired Fridays at midnight. Every Friday night Jae and I would sit next to each other in a conference room to watch the program we'd made that week. Emotions are contagious. Once I detected Jae's disillusionment with how we'd edited the pain of others for effect, I too started to feel guilty that everything I wrote was fake. As those Friday nights accumulated, I grew increasingly attuned to Jae's emotions and eventually discerned a new kind of suffering—disgust derived from helplessness—that I'd been oblivious to before meeting him. The program was intended to prompt a maximum number of viewers to call the ARS. Laudable on its face, this specific goal merely reflected the network's underlying dependency on ratings, a hunger we fed by sensationalizing personal tragedy and filling the narration with overblown emotions. When the episode ended and the theme music and end credits began, Jae and I would stare at each other. How could we have made such garbage? Neither of us blurted this out, but our eyes were shrouded with gloom.

Jae viewed pity as completely self-serving, as objectification of another's tragedy to achieve consolation for oneself. In a drunken state, he ranted that viewers pay a paltry dollar for a weekly reminder that their own life wasn't so bad. I couldn't agree. For me, the act of contemplating others and feeling their pain necessarily means negating selfish emotions, beliefs, and a preoccupation with one's own life. In grasping similarities between me and a person on the monitor, I am lifted up. Doubting and denying everything you thought you believed in, on the other hand, isolates and diminishes you. Meeting Jae is what crystallized these convictions.

As this crystal grew, my writing gradually changed. Connectives like "but" and "despite" grew more numerous, as did "we," "also," and "no different." Jae didn't offer even oblique compliments like "this script could work." He warned, rather, that while hope was okay, we shouldn't force it on our viewers. This observation betrayed a pessimistic belief that truthfulness and mass media are incompatible, and I wanted all the more to prove him wrong. My attitude toward the show's featured protagonists changed as well. I started meeting with them privately before shooting began, but not in formal recorded exchanges designed to facilitate my writing: casual and unhurried, these meetings unfolded over shared meals, where my only goal was to listen to their stories with an open mind. It was absurd now that I think about it. Reviewing the shooting plans proposed by junior writers, writing the episode, and revising it into final form already filled my week to capacity, to the point where I couldn't even stop to notice how busy I was. And yet, these absurdly impractical meetings where I would just listen became one of my most cherished routines.

And then I met Yunju.

Yunju was a seventeen-year-old high school girl who needed a protector but instead lived alone in a basement studio apartment. Her father had passed away three years before I met her, her mother had left years before that, and her sister had gone missing. Even with her hair covering most of her right cheek, she wouldn't lift her face to the world. I'd seen many who were unhappy, but something in Yunju moved my heart. What that something was, and whether my interest in her went overboard, I still struggle to understand. In any case, my interest in her story revealed the ruthlessness of my ambition.

Shooting resumed as Yunju's surgery date approached, but I had already decided on my own to reschedule the broadcast for the Chusok long weekend, when we could count on more viewers. We would air the episode at 11 p.m., so it would follow a popular entertainment show. Eleven o'clock at night is a better slot than midnight, and I'd calculated that increased family viewing would translate into more calls to the ARS. I didn't consult Yunju, but both Jae and Yunju's doctor agreed with my decision. And so Yunju's surgery was postponed for three months.

I thought everything would flow seamlessly.

"The first thing we did was remove tissue from the tumor and run a biopsy, and I'm afraid we have some bad news. The initial examination might have missed it, but in any case the tumor is malignant. And so we're looking at cancer and not a neurofibroma. These tumors rarely turn malignant so quickly . . . I'm so sorry."

So said the surgeon after the operation. Jae was asking him for a prognosis as he prepared to leave, and the staff who were scheduled to film Yunju post-op wore hollow looks. I was at a complete loss.

"I've been a doctor for over twenty years," the surgeon answered, "and this is a first. I just don't know what to say. We can't remove all of the tumor at this point. Maybe start with chemo to prevent metastasizing, but we'll need to do more tests."

The doctor continued to field Jae's questions, but his answers weren't registering in my mind. I was busy asking myself where God was in all this. Jae had once referred to God as a fantasy constructed by weak people anxious to perpetuate their existence. The remark came while filming a mother in her early twenties whose only instinct for her cancer-ridden daughter was to pray. Angered by his cynicism, I retorted that most people believe in God because they need momentary consolation, not eternal life. If one is consoled by praying to God, then so be it. But now I wasn't so sure. The unimaginable diagnosis had sent my thoughts topsy-turvy, and I could only feel bitter and furious toward a God who had dealt such a lot—to Yunju of all people.

Did things have to go that far, turn so disastrous . . .

That evening, submerging my head in a sink full of water in the hospital bathroom, I broke down. Yunju was still under anesthesia. I wanted to escape the pain Yunju would experience when, instead of a mirror image of her restored face, she was confronted with the biopsy result.

Self-doubt consumed me from that moment. Maybe I really did want to distance myself from Yunju and her impatient tumor, which couldn't wait three months before turning malignant. I began to wonder if my heart existed to serve me alone, while for others it had only hypocritical pity. My colleagues tried to comfort me: granted, I was the one who'd asked to postpone the surgery, but I had meant well, and no one, not even Yunju, could blame me. But in my ears it landed as mockery. Nor was there refuge in the implausibility that a neurofibroma had turned malignant in just three months. Even the likelihood that Yunju's tumor had already been cancerous by the time of the first biopsy—and therefore misdiagnosed—could not undo the choices I had made or the actions I had taken. Perhaps it was this persistent self-doubt, and not a fateful encounter with a sentence from an interview with North Korean refugees, that had brought me here.

The receptionist at Good Sleep Hostel stares at me blankly when I check out at the time I should be checking in without asking for a refund. I exit the hostel, pulling my suitcase behind.

Arriving at Pak's apartment, I leave the suitcase inside the door and sit down at the desk beside the living-room window. As I remove Loh's diary from my bag, I see its pages as an opportunity for self-reflection. I resolve to distinguish and balance genuine compassion and my own excruciating remorse—to seek confirmation, from myself rather than others, that neither Jae nor I was blameless.

December 10, 2010. Friday

I sit all day at the big wooden desk next to the living-room window, reading and rereading Loh's diary. Only when night falls do I close the cover, turn on my laptop, and open the music files I've downloaded. The first track is "Vocalise" by Rachmaninoff, and the next is "Knocking on Heaven's Door" by Bob Dylan.

When the tracks loop for the third time, I go to the fridge and take out a pilsner. Jae's two favorite drinks were warm sake and Czech pilsner. I loved rainy evenings in his living room savoring these drinks with jazz or blues playing. I used to think that even if tragic pain dominated the rest of my life, the occasional relaxing dinner over beer or sake with Jae would make it bearable.

Jae's momentous words from outside Yunju's hospital room are replaying in my head. They continue to weigh heavily on me.

I may convince myself that Jae's thoughts on pity are wrong, but I can't stop missing him. For five years we were almost perfect partners at work and something more in private. But never did we write or produce a scene that might reveal our feelings to each other. We were obsessive about being truthful, and perhaps we considered words too fickle and limiting. Truthful feelings are not created in a moment but emerge as a shared promise made with memories over time. Concrete events, prepared with care, must unfold though that time. Neither of us believed the word "love" was capable of encompassing all that; declaring we were now lovers would have felt childlike. I took comfort, rather, in the kind of mutual trust that only time can produce, in the relief you feel when you realize the person you're with is *the one,* and in shared tasks and routines that needed no explanation.

And yet.

After five years I still didn't know the true face of this person I worked with and saw almost every day. That time seems so far away now, a residue of images: the gray, pilled turtleneck sweater, the glasses with the black rims and smudged lenses, the dress shirts whose top buttons dangled precariously from a thread, the dark-brown suede sneakers with the shabby stitching.

The only certainty is that there's no recorded evidence of our feelings for each other and our time together. We may one day regret not complementing our dry and empty story with any sort of testament, worried as always about the limits of language even in confessing love. We will surely lament that all the self-censorship, the self-consciousness, the insistence on a pessimistic worldview that denies a belief in eternity were borne not of consideration for the other but of selfishness that flees one's innermost self. That mutual presentation of selves, indeed, was just like an edited film whose vast unsaid and unseen footage litters the cutting-room floor.

The most painful truth is that those editorial choices were our own.

The playlist has gone through seven loops. A third bottle of pilsner empties quickly, and my body, lately unaccustomed to drink, oozes lethargy and fatigue. I begin to lay myself down on the sofa but change my mind, return to the desk, and open Loh's diary again. A single ray of light from the bedside lamp reflects against my face as the bookmarked page opens. I see Loh's back as he sits on the bed inside the light, wetting his index finger to count his money. The light casts his swaying shadow deep into the room, where it beckons me to read and understand. I lean into the light and read Loh's anxiety and uneasiness one more time, tracing each line with my fingers.

Returning late in the evening to room 308 at Good Sleep Hostel, Loh locked the door, turned off the lights, and closed the curtains. Adjusting to darkness took time. He turned on a small bedside lamp, then blinked several times as his eyes adapted. He then reached into an inner pocket and removed a package wrapped in several layers of waterproof fabric. He never removed this item from his person except when showering. The money inside the wrapping, all that remained of his mother, caused a sharp pang every time he touched it.

The bills had deep wrinkles, and the sharp metal coins stung his hands. Loh counted each bill intently. But count as he may, inevitably, a handful of the money had disappeared since the previous day. Loh had to budget carefully. Hunger was a minor inconvenience he could easily endure and so too the gaiety of carousing backpackers from all over the world as they flocked from room to room late into the night. He needed to visit the South Korean embassy but kept putting it off, noting the trickle of expenditures that bought each delay. The embassy wouldn't necessarily solve all his problems. Who might have told him that? Another North Korean defector? The Korean-Chinese broker? Perhaps the warning had come from the South Korean missionaries he'd met in Yanji, who had encouraged him to go to Europe, a social welfare paradise that accepts illegal immigrants. The message, in any case, was clear: one should not expect too much from the South Korean embassy. The thought left Loh scared. I can't forgive the rash person who had played up the limitations of what was surely Loh's only recourse, directing him to this lonesome hostel for ten long days. Was the advice just nearsighted, or was the person incapable of compassion?

Staring blankly as he sat on the bed, Loh started to rewrap his bills and coins. Through his journal I watch him perform this ritual by lamplight. And I realize suddenly that Loh—someone I've neither seen nor spoken to—now occupies a space in my life and that despite my original intentions, his progress now holds me in thrall. "L." is no longer a code that beckons me into a new world. It has become a spell leading me deeper into my own life.

The familiar scene returns.

Your tumor is malignant. I'm sorry.

Yunju must have heard this as she emerged from anesthesia to confront excruciating pain and clouded consciousness. A message neither warm nor cold, just the dispassionate words of medicine and business. A reality that can't be changed and doesn't admit alternatives. Yunju was alone at the time. I remained in the restroom, Jae paced nervously outside, and the staff had canceled filming and returned home.

Yunju would have turned toward the windows after her doctor left. In my imagination I enter her room and observe a girl who has been cast into the darkest, loneliest, most anxious moment of her life. I leave out the scene in which I run—much too late—to her room after hearing she's come to and am told "Go away" in a dry, calm voice. I also edit out my foolish decision to heed those words and walk away immediately. I wish I could erase all of those scenes. When I closed the door behind me, Yunju was alone again.

From that day on, I avoided her.

I needed a place to escape from the self-doubt that tortured and consumed me. I didn't want to sigh and weep in the presence of a seventeen-year-old girl who, because of me, was locked in a battle she could never win. Nor did I want to justify myself by hiding behind those emotions. Every day I found it more of a struggle to see her at the hospital, though I knew full well she often cried when left alone and that she had no family or friends to visit her.

When she hit bottom, she would lash herself with words, and it must have been a shock when she realized the things she'd said. And there I was, running away from it all. Confined in her solitary space, Yunju must have recalled her father, who had devoted long stretches to wallowing in misery after his back injury. He had lost interest in returning to society and spent his remaining days drinking and abusing his family until, finally, he passed away. She may have felt suicidal when she saw her father in herself, the father she hated just enough not to kill. At least once I should have allowed her to cry her heart out in my arms. But when I peeked in and found her muttering to herself, I cruelly turned away instead.

Each time I turned away, and whenever her medical team left her alone, Yunju inevitably resumed her solitary battle with her own demons.

December 12, 2010. Sunday

The morning started with rain. The temperature plunged, rain changed to snow, then snow became rain again. The result is something half frozen, neither rain nor snow, and it permeates the city of Brussels. My umbrella can't prevent my winter coat from quickly getting soaked through in the wet wind. I walk diligently, savoring the warmth of an Americano I bought.

I arrive at the restaurant to see Pak seated beneath a parasol, having a coffee and a smoke. The restaurant is near De Brouckère subway station. I check my cell phone—I'm ten minutes early. How long has Pak been waiting outside the restaurant?

Two nights ago I drank myself tipsy with the remaining pilsner in the fridge. Several times I turned on my cell phone, only to turn it off without making a call, and all the while Pak was on my mind. He and the reporter were the only two people I could meet in this city, but since the reporter would be busy, why risk a breach of etiquette by calling him? Anyway, from the moment I took my phone in hand I was thinking of Pak.

"Rain's stopped," says Pak as I hurry toward the parasol. Only now do I realize scarcely anyone else is using an umbrella. I fold mine and stash it in my bag. "Shall we walk?"

I nod at Pak's suggestion and offer to help him out of his seat. Pak declines with a discreet wave of the hand, gets to his feet, and sets off a few steps ahead of me. As with our first meeting, we walk in silence. After a while I ask the name of the street we're on.

"Rue au Beurre. *Beurre* means 'butter' in French. There are quite a few interesting street names in this country. Nearby we have Cheese Street and Herb Street."

I have to laugh.

Almost every page of Loh's diary is littered with street names written in the Latin alphabet. Whenever he encountered a new street, he looked up at the sign and wrote the name on a scrap of napkin or the back of a McDonald's receipt. Rue du Lavoir, Rue de la Forge, Rue des Bouchers, Rue Longue Vie, Rue du Clocher, Rue au Bois, Rue Piers, Rue des Charbonniers . . . Loh preferred walking south on Rue Neuve, turning onto Rue du Fossé aux Loups, then taking a right at Rue d'Arenberg. But not always. One day he took Rue de l'Ecuyer and not Rue d'Arenberg and stayed on it until he reached Gare Centrale. Another day he walked to Gare du Nord, where he'd arrived his first day here, then took Rue Dupont. Recording street names was an important part of his daily routine, and each evening after he counted his money, he transcribed the names from his scattered memos onto the pages of the diary, checking them against a map of the city just to be sure. Aside from the English name of his country, Loh probably had few chances to write in English. The neatness of his diary entries reveals the time and effort he spent on each letter. As one entry noted, he also wanted to write the street names in the order he encountered them.

Why would he devote so much care to recording these names?

He would have been concerned about getting lost, but there was more to it than that. He may have considered the street names his only tangible proof that he lived in Brussels. Loh hadn't exchanged even a simple greeting with anyone on these streets. A diminutive, slightly built Asian man was easy to spot, but no one was curious as to how he'd ended up here, and no one seemed inclined to converse with him. This city was impassive to all this particular human being had experienced—his nationality, which had become irrelevant, and his mother tongue, the language he could speak unrestrained. He must have occasionally noticed his image in shop windows that reflected a busy, preoccupied world—people imprinted with a homing instinct, emergency vehicles with blaring horns speeding past, pigeons overhead transporting furtive messages to secret recipients, each of them with a destination and a reason for living. Overlapping those images was the faint, ghostly silhouette of Loh himself.

Loh often frequented Grand-Place, a tourist attraction in downtown Brussels. More precisely, whether he headed north or south during the day, he always returned to the hostel along a street that led to Grand-Place. If Rue Neuve shocked Loh with its affluence and capitalism, Grand-Place and the city center overwhelmed him with their refined historic buildings—the antique façades; the delicate, enigmatic sculptures beside a column or under a roof; the beautiful terraces from which someone would wave to you in welcome. When dusk fell, the city slowly lit up, and Loh imagined all manner of luminescent moths waking from their daytime slumber to flutter through the streets. To his eyes, every building was beautiful. But the light from this strange, dream-like place would soon fade as cold and hunger reasserted themselves. Try as he might to keep it at bay with his brisk pace, the biting chill at his extremities soon commanded his attention, and he would have to seek shelter in a shop, canvassing items as if he were a customer. Not a single clerk ever asked if he needed help finding something.

It's the Christmas season, and small stalls shaped like log houses line Rue au Beurre. Decorated with white balls of cotton and red lights, they look even more diminutive, like fairy dwellings whose winter magic is spaghetti, barbecue, crepes, sausages, sandwiches, and mulled wine. Pak asks if I'm hungry.

Not hungry, I answer playfully, but joining the crowds standing at the stalls with their plates of food and glasses of wine would be fun. We walk up to a stall and order two cheese crepes at five euros each. I cut through the crepe and eat, and my eyes meet Pak's. The snow has started again, and white flakes have settled on his gray hair, his thick glasses, and his ash-colored trench coat. His big eyes, hidden safely behind the thick lenses, blink when I smile at his snow-covered form.

Loh walked this street three years ago during the Christmas season, before he visited the South Korean embassy, an agonizing ten-day stretch when a small hope of help from the embassy fought with a conviction that he shouldn't expect much. Food was cheaper at the stalls than in restaurants or bars, and he ate here several times. Did he have spaghetti? Sausage? Would he even have known what he was eating? Buying food at an outdoor stall must have been a new experience for him in any case. I stop chewing my crepe long enough to imagine Loh's face as he stared at menus displayed outside the myriad restaurants in Brussels. I imagine too the enormous resolve that prevented him from entering any of them. Not a single person beckoned Loh inside from where he lingered.

As Pak and I drink mulled wine from another stall, he tells me that in Europe in winter, mulled wine is ubiquitous, like coffee. Maybe it's the warming that leaves the wine tasting less sweet and stronger than I expected. In no time I feel my cheeks turning red, and now it's Pak who laughs silently at me. And it hits me that it's been ages since I've been with someone without feeling self-conscious or socially awkward. Pak too? As we resume our stroll, he whispers, barely audible, "This is nice."

Pak and I pass Gare de Bruxelles-Chapelle. Somewhere around here Loh witnessed a protest, a first for him in this city. He was walking on the avenue between Gare de Bruxelles-Chapelle and South Station when a sudden crescendo of voices and music brought him to a stop.

It was around 2 p.m., Tuesday, December 11, 2007. I searched the Internet but found no details of a protest on that date; perhaps small protests were too frequent back then to draw media coverage. There was only an article noting sporadic protests—some in opposition to Turkey joining the European Union and others, organized by the labor unions, criticizing the government's labor policies—that took place across Belgium during the winter of 2007. It was probably one such protest that Loh witnessed.

Loh saw people in green shirts and blue jeans trailing colorful balloons as they followed a sedan that played rhythmic music. The atmosphere was cheerful and festive—no violence, no yelling, just people dancing; a few even embraced or kissed. Loh was unsure whether they were really demonstrating or simply throwing a party. A person out in front would shout something through a megaphone, and the crowd would repeat the phrase while several people held up placards and flags with messages in primary colors. The police were out, some keeping to the sidewalks and maintaining radio contact while others with a luminous *X* on their vests diverted traffic. Loh was astonished: How could ordinary people come together as a group to oppose government policy by voicing their opinions and dancing and singing to cheerful, uplifting music?

Was there really a hell on Earth?

From where he stood observing the march, Loh recalled a sermon on that topic at a Korean church in Yanji.

Loh's mother had attended that church diligently, not because it promised salvation but because the anxieties of being uprooted created a need to depend on something. The missionaries from South Korea were generally kind but also shallow. Despite their enticing rhetoric that genuine freedom was to be found in their country, the promises came with strings attached: offers of help with food and housing seemed to go only to those willing to tour South Korean churches, confess their encounter with God, and expose the stark tragedies of life in North Korea. But when Loh approached the missionaries and made direct appeals, they retreated.

Loh attended a few services at the urging of his mom but never became a regular, and he felt hostile toward the people he met at the church. He couldn't bring himself to believe in God, especially after witnessing people die of starvation. He stopped going altogether after the sermon in which the minister described North Korea as pure hell, insisting that the poor lambs there must be rescued immediately. Loh acknowledged that his country was poor but never thought of it as hell. What is hell, he wanted to ask. If poverty is hell, then hell exists throughout capitalism. Perhaps in capitalist countries only some experience hell, while the systematic hell in his country swallows up vast multitudes. That would be the only difference, Loh used to think. If his country were wealthy and mighty, it would gladly have shown mercy to all. Loh despised those who condemned his country—one that was ready to share everything if only it had anything to share—when they themselves had so much but balked and ran off when the moment to share arrived.

Watching the crowd march freely in Brussels, though, Loh began to register tiny fractures in his belief system. For one thing, although his country had offered him a good—albeit poor—community, it was also ruthlessly cruel to those who questioned or rejected the supposed good intentions of the regime.

For those who did not learn resistance, poverty grew so familiar and pervasive that few could think of it more abstractly as a systemic flaw or failing of the country's leader. Not that fear of punishment prevented them; there simply wasn't enough information to compare different countries and acquire perspective on one's own. Most of all, though, the luxury of pondering alternatives wasn't available to those whose daily toil barely kept them alive. In Seseon Village, where Loh grew up, people ate the bark of nearby trees and then cut the trees down for fuel. Hunger pushed people to harvest greens before they could ripen. Many attempted to sell their own necessities at the market place, and these might take ages to sell. But no one ran out into the streets shouting antigovernment slogans or tried to agitate. People just waited quietly in hopes that the old days of simple abundance would soon return—days when they'd received their rations on schedule, when schools had always had enough supplies, and new clothes would arrive on annual holidays. The realization that no one had taken responsibility for that long wait for a resurgent utopia tortured Loh as he watched the protest in Brussels. That lack of responsibility had caused him to migrate with his mother across the river to China, where he'd confined himself in a small room to avoid raids by the Chinese police. It had led, finally, to him using funds from the loss of his mother toward a journey to Belgium, a country whose name he'd only just learned. Loh recalled all the incomprehensible happenings since he'd left home. He pondered how both people in the system and those observing it kept equally silent despite the interminable waiting and the many who perished as a result. His goal had simply been to live out his life; instead he'd wound up in limbo between different countries and systems, lacking a foothold in any of them. With this jarring displacement came a reckoning that from now on, nostalgia alone wouldn't revive sweet memories of home.

Loh resumed walking, the only thing he could do in this city.

Was that day, December 11, three years ago, cold like today, fluctuating between rain and snow?

"Antiabortion and opposed to euthanasia. Must be Catholics."

Several people are gathered at a table in front of Gare du Midi, playing guitars and singing. Others display signs, hand out flyers to pedestrians, and solicit signatures on a petition against abortion and euthanasia. Pak comes to a stop. Standing beside him I read the signs. I hear Pak whisper to himself that it's useless.

"You don't oppose abortion and euthanasia and yet you're Catholic?"

"Is that what the reporter told you?"

"He mentioned it, yes."

"As for the abortion issue, I'm in no position to speak. I don't have direct experience."

"But there has to be a reason for dissent, whether it's abortion or euthanasia."

"A reason for dissent, for euthanasia—do you realize what you're saying?"

I flinch. I've offended Pak. Why is he so sensitive about euthanasia?

"Since we're on the topic, let me ask. What do you think of euthanasia, Kim *chakka?*"

"Well . . ."

I struggle for words. I've heard that euthanasia is legal in Belgium, as in Switzerland and Holland. But I've never thought about it seriously. I know the term, but to me it's just an institutional abstraction that has nothing to do with my life.

"A year or so ago," Pak continues, "I happened to see a Korean news program—the respirator was about to be removed from a patient in a vegetative state, and the country was in an uproar. These people you see here aren't protesting the right to die with dignity, which is what the Korean case was all about. They're opposed to assisted death—death from an injection prescribed by a doctor."

"Is *this* something you have direct experience with?"

"Me?"

Pak stares at me intently. I feel I've inadvertently entered a forbidden area, a secret space in which Pak feels fragile. He answers after a pause.

"When I was practicing in France, they brought in a twenty-four-year-old man who'd been paralyzed from the neck down in a car crash. When he woke from his coma and realized he was a quadriplegic, he asked for the injection. I said no. Euthanasia was illegal in France, and general paralysis, devastating though it may be for the patient, is not necessarily fatal—and it has to be fatal for the doctor to write the prescription. The next time I saw him was three years later, in the newspaper. He died in a car fire. Suicide, needless to say. By then he weighed less than a hundred pounds, and this was a man who was almost six feet tall. Boom. Something exploded inside me: I realized I'd withheld a drug that would have allowed him to die in relative comfort. Instead, I prescribed him three years of what had to be horrific stress and excruciating pain. Until then I'd never doubted myself as a doctor.

"And then, five years ago, I had another patient. She had end-stage liver cancer. The liver is what we call a 'silent' organ. It's one of the largest, but it doesn't fuss until it goes bad, and by then it's too late to do anything. I knew that patient, and I understood her wishes better than anyone. She wanted to die clean. So I let her, without anyone knowing. I closed my practice right after that, but I have no regrets."

This is Pak's longest narrative since we've met. I can't immediately process it and bide my time by pretending to remain detached.

"Without anyone knowing—is that possible?"

"I made it possible."

I feel my eyes widen as a sudden chill descends over me.

The snow has stopped, leaving the street a slushy mess. In that moment Pak's profile has turned unrecognizable. Who is he? What kind of person am I talking to? *Without anyone knowing.* I repeat the phrase to myself. How is that any different from murder?

"Where would you like to go next?" he asks tiredly, without looking in my direction. We don't have a destination, and I can't come up with an answer. All I can do is continue to stare at his profile.

"If it's okay with you, I'd like to head home." Saying this, he removes his glasses and presses down on his temples with his right thumb and index finger. "I'm tired," he mumbles in a voice steeped in fatigue. I tell him I'd like to walk him to the subway station, but he politely declines. He says to contact him any time I have more to ask about Loh Kiwan, then turns quickly and heads toward Gare du Midi. Doesn't Pak know we didn't say a word about Loh? Not that it was my primary purpose in seeing him today.

I stroll a bit longer around Gare du Midi. The area is notorious for pickpockets and beggars. One often spots young men hunting for a bag to snatch and Gypsies asking for change. Teenagers laugh and banter among themselves, their words sounding like slang. A black man wearing earphones looks at the sky and mutters something. A young white woman has bright red eyes—from alcohol perhaps. Some Arabs look wary—a rock or a bullet?—as they cross the street. Where to? As I ponder this, my brain reminds me that the Korean embassy in Belgium, next on my itinerary, lies somewhere ahead. But my wavering heart finds comfort in postponing the visit as long as I can, just as Loh did. Doing so assures me that I'm on the right path—that I'm not just retracing Loh's route but also embracing his loneliness and unease as I drift about the city.

I redirect myself toward the apartment Pak has lent me. I need to find the exact location of the embassy anyway.

December 14, 2010. Tuesday

A desolate scene replays in my mind.

Twenty Asians have gathered in the Berlin airport: eighteen Chinese, one North Korean defector, and a Korean-Chinese broker who leads the group. All wear blank expressions, and the hands clutching their big bags are rough from years of manual labor. They've just disembarked from a Boeing 747 arriving from Qingdao, China, by way of Hong Kong. With anxious glances and racing hearts that pound beneath the casual veneer of their shabby clothes, they pass uneventfully through immigration. The first gate on their adventure closes slowly behind them.

Outside the port of entry, they gather for a bemused farewell, the second gate on their journey. From this point on, they'll each face their challenges alone. What has led them to this foreign way station, abandoning their nationality to venture into the unknown in search of the hope lost at home? How did they choose the destinations whose names now pulse in their minds: Germany, England, France, Holland, Sweden, Norway? What events convinced them to take such a momentous risk that, for better or worse, will shape the rest of their lives? Have they navigated into this vast unknown through the comforting simplicity of a roll of the dice?

The parting is quiet and forlorn. The Korean-Chinese broker goes among his people, retrieving the forged South Korean passports given upon their departure from China and returning their Chinese passports. Loh, lacking a Chinese passport to start with, gets nothing returned to him and instead toys with the handle of his bag. The others pat each other on the shoulders or hug half-heartedly before going their own way. No one looks back, despite the uncertainty about whether the road ahead leads to settlement or deportation. They're painfully aware that the sum of their preparations—a passport without a legal visa tucked away in an inner coat pocket, just enough money to cover a few days' food and accommodation, bus or train tickets provided by the broker—can guarantee only temporary help, if any at all. Loh alone remains, the only North Korean member of the group.

Loh watches from a short distance as the Chinese scatter. He too had picked a country before leaving China, but it was a blind choice. The names of European countries—Germany, England, France, Holland, Sweden, Norway, etcetera—only confused him. He had little sense of where they were, and none of his relatives or extended family lived there. He wonders where the Chinese are headed and what hopes they have for their chosen destinations. If any had turned and invited Loh to come along, he would have grabbed his bag and joined them. But he just stands there amid the bustle, apprehensive and cut off, with nowhere to go and no place to return to.

"Go to Belgium," the broker says in a low voice. As soon as his people disperse, the broker is supposed to retreat to a reserved hotel room and return to China the next day. Instead he approaches Loh with this suggestion. Belgium? Loh asks, and the broker tells him it's a small country, but international organizations are headquartered there, and the Belgians don't go around arresting people for no good reason. It also has a good social welfare system, he adds; applying for refugee status might be easier there. Loh nods gratefully, clinging to the broker's words, a lifeline to a place he'd barely heard of. The broker gives him a guidebook, then writes down an address for the South Korean embassy in Belgium. Loh studies the letters and words while the broker buys him a bus ticket to Brussels at the Euroline office near the airport. They don't inspect passports when you cross the border by bus, he explains. He also notes that Brussels is the capital of Belgium and that most of the people speak French and Flemish, as well as English. Loh bows repeatedly in gratitude, but the broker just says, "Stay alive and we'll meet again sometime."

The words reverberate, echoing the silent will of Loh's mother. Survival was Loh's sole objective when he left Yanji. The broker gives Loh a handful of coins—they'll come in handy in Belgium. Then he rummages through his bag, retrieves a passport, and places it in Loh's hand. The forged South Korean passport the broker had just taken from Loh a short time ago.

"You may find it useful, even though it's fake."

Loh's eyes brim as he gazes at the broker, who gives Loh's shoulder a firm squeeze. Loh places the slip of paper with the address for the South Korean embassy in his inner pocket. When he looks up again, the broker has disappeared into the crowd.

Loh stands for some time outside the airport, searching desperately for some scrap of familiarity in an environment of utter strangeness and abandonment, where people and objects and even his own plans seem part of a different universe. Again and again he checks his bus ticket, but it gives no clue as to whether it leads to security and stability or trouble and further flight. Surviving, Loh realizes, will depend on things beyond his control. He seems oblivious to the cold as he stands there, rubbing his eyes to hold back fatigue and jet lag. Like a mantra, he articulates the names of the country and city where he'll soon arrive—*bel-gi-um-bru-ssels bel-gi-um-bru-ssels.* He knows nothing about them—not their location, size, history, or religion. Finally, he reties his shoelaces and grabs his bag. Time to get to the second gate, where a Euroline bus departs shortly for Brussels.

Was the broker's hand warm on Loh's shoulder? Did it offer solace, at least at that moment? I can't say; this is as far as my imagination takes me.

December 15, 2010. Wednesday

Chaussée de la Hulpe 175, 1170 Brussels, Belgium
Tel: (32–2) 675–5777
Take Tram #94 to Herrmann-Debroux at Louise subway station and get off at Coccinelles. Sixteen tram stops, 30 min. from Louise station.

Would the broker have written down directions such as this? The place-names would have been written in the Latin alphabet, and the phone number might have been missing. It's impossible to know how much the broker accommodated Loh's limited facility with the alphabet or whether he used the liner from a pack of cigarettes or perhaps the back of a ticket to jot down the information. I don't have the piece of paper, which Loh would have guarded as carefully as he did the money wrapped in waterproof cloth. What I do know is that the sentence "Need to visit embassy tomorrow" appears several times in Loh's journal.

The streets must have been splendid as Christmas approached, and a festive joy would have permeated the foreign tourists staying at the hostels. With the last stage of his journey lying ahead, Loh spent ten days strolling around Brussels, thinking of the directions to the embassy, counting his remaining money, writing down street names, and dealing with guilt over his mother. He half expected the embassy to offer help; was half convinced they'd turn him away. For those ten days, Loh swung between the highs of expectation and the depths of despair. Looking out of tram 94 from beneath his cap, he would have brooded for the whole trip.

When I emerge from Louise station, tram 94 is already there. I race to the stop and catch it. The tram departs, and soon the city center and its capitalist dazzle fade from view. In their place appear rows of low-rise residences, shabby buildings whose use is hard to guess, walls decorated with graffiti, and parks with no people. Dusk is blooming when I arrive at Coccinelles, by the embassy.

Loh's bad luck waited with the patience of destiny.

The embassy staff explained the policy: With no evidence that Loh had escaped North Korea, they cannot help him apply for refugee status. Despite all the setbacks he'd faced until now, Loh was momentarily baffled at the cold words. The documentation his mother had prepared for both of them before they crossed the river—national identification cards, birth certificates, Loh's student card, all issued by the regime—of course she'd relinquished these documents. Papers from their native country became useless once they'd renounced it and might have put them at mortal risk if found by the Chinese police. Loh desperately explained all of this, but the staff took it as a common deception. They kept watch for Korean-Chinese who, with fluent North Korean accents, would contact the South Korean embassy and the Belgian Ministry of the Interior posing as defectors. These impostors knew that submitting an application for refugee status would gain them temporary housing and free language classes and that approval of refugee status guaranteed them a minimum living allowance and job allocation services.

The embassy staff may have turned Loh away thinking he was Korean-Chinese. But even had he proved himself a North Korean defector, that very fact meant he wasn't a South Korean citizen and thus was out of their jurisdiction. Loh knew he had to leave but stood frozen in place until two men appeared and ushered him out. The staff returned to their desks and immersed themselves in their work; no one showed pity as Loh walked away. Loh loitered outside the embassy for a time. He'd risked his life crossing borders, lost the most precious person in the world, and drifted into yet another foreign country just to stay alive. And now that journey had amounted to nothing. Loh stumbled at the bottom of the embassy staircase as this new reality came crashing down.

The gate is locked—past business hours, perhaps. Even if the gate were open and I chanced upon the same staff who had dealt with Loh, there's nothing I could say. If asked my relation to Loh, I might tell them I was learning about his life through reading his journal. But while that response would explain my purpose, what could I then expect from them? From a bureaucratic point of view, no connection between Loh and me exists that would make sense or elicit an administrative response.

Loh walked a short distance, stopped, resumed walking, then collapsed onto the sidewalk. Imagining someone contending with so much bad luck pierces me to the core. Up to this point, my sadness was somehow abstract, a nascent potential. But in that moment it turns visceral, a fire of flesh-and-blood despair that consumes my heart. Loh struggled to raise himself and staggered aimlessly. My footsteps in his wake likewise grow erratic and weak.

Only when he reached a lonesome alley did Loh lean against a wall, bend over double, and wail. I stand at the alley's entrance and watch, riveted and helpless, as a person spews out tears.

Yunju was all by herself, crying.

I couldn't open the door to the sickroom, merely waited for the tears to end. Sometimes people can't offer needed comfort because even the most sincere attempt at consolation ends up summoning cheap pity instead. Reflecting on that moment now, I grasp how two strangers, worlds apart and unaware of the other's existence, may nonetheless be bound by a deep, inconsolable sorrow.

I waited and waited, but Yunju wouldn't stop crying. She would have if she'd known I was there—she never cried in front of me, either before or after learning her tumor was malignant. She felt that shedding tears posed an unnecessary burden on others and I understood that. Perhaps my interest in her and my tendency to see myself in her reflected Yunju's foolhardy patience and cool attitude toward herself. Ever since adolescence I too have kept myself dry-eyed with others. And that included Jae. A French philosopher once wrote that the act of crying in the presence of a loved one proves that one's pain is not a fantasy. Extrapolating that statement to relationships in general, I now realize that I didn't cry in front of others because I knew my pain was a fantasy. I could easily imagine both the physical response and the relief I would experience from shedding those tears, so I censored my grief because I decided it was not truthful. Honesty, sincerity, genuineness. Is it possible that Yunju, Jae, and I had lost too much to be able to safeguard these virtues, assuming they even exist in this world?

It's impossible to know exactly where Loh leaned against the wall and cried. I walk unsteadily for a time but can't recover the searing image of a moment ago and finally lose energy and slump down, spent. I feel only that I too want to cry at this spot. In this alien land with no family or colleague to share the moment, wearing a foreigner's veil, lacking warm encouragement from anyone, I turn my lingering gaze inward.

Yunju was for me a blend of hope and despair, as the embassy was for Loh. But I can't clearly discern what I hope for her and what I despair of. A belief that Yunju will eventually forgive me and a foreboding that she never will—I don't know which of the two I really hope for. Which do I need more desperately: to be unburdened with a pardon, or to be rightly refused exoneration?

Only when it was time to leave for the airport did I try to reach her.

And against all expectation, she took my call. Even more surprising, she started by asking me where I was just then. Perhaps Jae had given her an update, saying I planned to be abroad for a spell. Yunju probably knew where I was headed, but I mentioned Brussels anyway and prattled on about having to leave soon for the airport while at the same time assuring her I was in no rush since it was an evening flight. From the second-floor balcony, I could see Yunju directing her wheelchair toward the hospital entry, but then she frowned ever so slightly.

She occasionally used the wheelchair now that her chemotherapy was making itself felt, but to me it seemed more like an instrument of punishment than a means of patient mobility. Looking down at Yunju wheeling her torture machine past the lobby, I asked as dispassionately as I could if I might visit. Yunju came to a stop, looking as if she'd lost her composure.

"Don't you want to see me?" I asked. But the dare didn't work.

Yunju was silent for a moment and then said, "I'm busy right now."

"I see. Well, I figured as much," I responded after a short pause. A hand went to my chest. Neither of us spoke again right away, but we weren't ready to end the call, either.

"Well, when do you think you'll be back?" Yunju ventured. Maybe she wanted to change the topic.

"I haven't decided," I said, after another short pause. I couldn't tell her I was sorry I wouldn't be there for her imminent surgery. If this operation brought another disappointment, I would lose the inner conflict between wanting a pardon and shunning its very possibility—a conflict that had sustained me. But I couldn't tell her that, either. I couldn't confess to the person facing surgery that I was trying to escape its results. I knew not to show my brutal fragility. After a short silence, Yunju calmly responded that the trip would be a good experience for my writing. An apt pleasantry for one who has written for television and is embarking on a trip. The words were obvious, insignificant, and devoid of warmth—worse than "See you when you get back" or "Be sure to call me."

And then the call was over. I don't remember who said good-bye first.

What was I expecting? I asked myself this question over and over as I left the hospital, rode to the airport, and waited for boarding to begin. It torments me to this moment.

"Don't forgive him," Jae advised me after I told him self-consciously about a broken relationship. We were at a sake bar we frequented in Kwanghwamun. I was having warm sake, from time to time blowing across the surface of the liquid to cool it down.

"What do you mean?" I asked.

"I mean don't let him off the hook. Keep hating him like a normal human being. Hate is a fierce emotion, and it's his farewell present to you." I gave him a sharp glance, then grinned.

I'll have to take his advice again, this time changing the object of contempt. I, the one who turned tail and ran from the hospital that day, am the one to hate. I deserve to be hated by myself. As I went down the stairs to the ground floor, I knew instinctively that Yunju saw me. But I didn't look her way. I merely hastened across the lobby, pushed open the glass door, and rushed out into the bright winter daylight.

The truth is, I hoped Yunju would not forgive me. As sorry as I was that she hated me, her enduring hatred, a kind of penance for me, would unburden me of my guilt. The moment this penance was removed, the rest of my life would be consumed with self-loathing.

December 16, 2010. Thursday

The woman in jeans at Good Sleep Hostel remembers me from a week ago. It's probably not common for a guest to ask for a particular room, not stay the night, not ask for a refund, and then check out. Like the last time, she's chewing gum. She asks if I want room 308 again.

"No, I'd like the dormitory. How much would that be?"

Three years ago it was sixteen euros.

"Eighteen euros." A two-euro increase in just three years. I take out my wallet and pay the amount. In an indifferent tone, she advises me that the room is available after three o'clock, like the last time.

It's noon when I leave the hostel. At the McDonald's at 24 Rue Neuve, I order coffee, take it to the same window seat as last time, and add two packets of sugar. I plan to eat nothing until tomorrow, and the best thing for enduring hours of hunger is sugar. I look out the window as I sip the extra-sweet brew, a departure from my usual preference with coffee.

Loh switched to a dormitory room after his hopes were dashed at the South Korean embassy. He had 118.52 euros left in the waterproof wrap. Not enough to last a week even if he went nowhere, starved himself, and slept in the dormitory room. He needed a job. Knowing that without identification or language skills—he'd never studied French or English—one can't get a job even in a small factory or a grocery store, Loh clung to hope nonetheless. He also found himself abandoning it. As in Yanji, he knew he couldn't expect to earn a living.

Thoughts of the violin player and the vagrants he'd encountered near the stations and in the underpasses kept cropping up. Inevitably, he took to imagining himself on the street, begging pedestrians for change. After he managed to dispel the gloom he felt at such a prospect, he was able to consider the practicalities of begging. In his bag was a harmonica. He'd learned to play it at his elementary school in Seseon and before long could play a melody that extolled the Great Leader and wished him good health and long life. Elementary school was for four years, but due to forces beyond his control, he had only attended for three.

In 1995, the year after he started elementary school, deluges and epidemics swept North Korea. Reduced support from the Soviet Union and China, shrunken trade brought on by the collapse of Eastern European communism, land devastated by the overuse of fertilizer, a failure to industrialize agriculture due to fuel shortages, and decades of American economic sanctions and trade deficits worked together like a giant siege engine, giving the country no way to sustain itself. And 1995 was just the beginning. Floods struck the following year, followed by a tsunami and drought in 1997. In 1998 a typhoon devastated the whole country. During this time, now called the Arduous March, two to three million North Koreans were reported to have starved to death. Those who wanted the regime to collapse—the United States, the West, South Korea—withheld food aid during the height of the starvation, and the regime feared the demise of what it boasted to the outside was a "paradise on Earth." In this calculating, coldhearted political game, any issue that was private and individual, such as a student's right to learn, became inconsequential. No political stratagem gave weight to the teary eyes of parents who watched their children starve, or the soiled hands of begging orphans, or the regrets of a middle-aged woman who beat a young boy she'd caught stealing food from her only to collapse at the memory of her own son's death from malnutrition. The scarcity of school supplies made school a luxury; and besides, the teachers were gone. It wasn't just the names of the dead that historical records ignored: even their nameless, anonymous number had no commemorating plaque. The tears and disillusionment of survivors likewise went unnoticed.

I entered university in the year 1995. I read about the conditions in North Korea in postings on the campus bulletin board. I belonged to a generation that, while not exactly disinterested in politics or social concerns, also wasn't defined by activism. I lingered before the postings but casually passed by the donation boxes. My young life already knew poverty, though not to a degree that threatened my very survival, the way it did for those in the photographs I passed. A photograph of Loh, eight or nine years old and starving, would have belonged there. Neither of us could have known then that in the future we'd be taking parallel journeys three years apart. A violent indifference returns. Who am I to criticize those who told Loh not to expect much from the embassy? I drain my coffee, get to my feet, and head to the restroom on the second floor.

Loh often used this McDonald's restroom because it was free. Unlike at other restaurants and franchises in Brussels, one can use the restrooms here without having to make a purchase. I close the toilet seat lid and sit. The restroom is clean enough but not a place to be eating.

Breakfast at the hostel is from eight to nine in the mornings. Loh never missed it. An empty stomach prevented him from sleeping in, and he was up before six to wash, brush his teeth, get dressed, and tidy his hair. He would have wanted to avoid appearing destitute and figured no one there would understand the pain of hunger.

Even after all these preparations, eight o'clock still seemed an eternity to wait. Finally, an unhurried-looking ten or twenty minutes past eight, he went down to the cafeteria on the second floor. He would have yearned to snatch pastries and milk from the shelves and cooler and pile them on his tray, but he forced himself to remain calm. He would have kept his poise while eating as well. His journal reveals someone cautious and wary of others, who doesn't act rashly and keeps a low profile. Loh didn't pretend he wasn't hungry but simply tried to pass for a young tourist who, like most of the hostel guests, enjoyed life and leisure.

After his meal Loh placed the food he'd purposely left uneaten in his pockets. With the embassy having extinguished his last hopes, squirreling away food had become more important than writing down street names. He took time to collect individually wrapped packets of butter and jam, hoping to give the impression that he simply liked the hostel's rolls and not that he couldn't afford the condiments. Did anyone buy this act? Wouldn't the busing staff and some of the cosmopolitan young tourists have scowled at his brazenness? Loh must have looked odd indeed with his bulging pockets, but he maintained the ruse until he'd left the cafeteria. It isn't written in his journal, but I can feel the torment in his heart whenever he had to do this. But he couldn't stop: he'd long since experienced how overpowering hunger can be.

He'd stopped growing at age fifteen.

The rolls, butter, and jam stuffed in his pockets were his provisions for the day. Around two in the afternoon, Loh would visit this free restroom, lock the door, sit down on the toilet lid, and take a roll from his pocket. His hands would grow impatient as they spread jam and butter. Then he'd gulp the roll with no water to wash it down and maybe lick the jam and butter packets clean. In this confined and lonely space, hunger gnawing his insides, Loh came face to face with his destitute state. Despite indulging in tears over his predicament, Loh made sure to save one of the rolls.

I've brought a jam sandwich in a Ziploc bag from Pak's apartment, but I can't bring myself to eat it. I look down at the two slices of bread I can neither eat nor throw out, then raise the sandwich to my lips and gnaw on the corner. I gag immediately. Steeling myself, I stuff the whole thing in my mouth and start chewing. A few bites along I rise, open the toilet lid, and spit everything into the bowl. I loathe my body's incapacity to stomach Loh's experience and truly confront the misery he endured.

At three o'clock I drag my tired body back to the hostel.

Four of the beds remain unclaimed. I leave my suitcase by a window, walk to the sink, turn on the water, and drink from my hands. The first thing Loh used to do once he returned here was drink from the tap. Thirst quenched, he would lay himself out on his bed. He'd stopped his evening strolls. Like a hapless organism that has degenerated into mere survival in the dark, insensate to pleasure or joy, sometimes deriding himself that his extreme yearning for life too often put everything at risk, Loh would eventually fall into a fitful sleep. And except for a brief rally around seven in the evening, when he consumed the last roll from his daily stash, he stayed in bed. He had to conserve energy.

~

On a rainy Wednesday evening, Loh was in bed, rolled up in a blanket. On the other side of a rickety wall, young tourists were indulging themselves in chatting, drinking, and laughter. Noise from their merriment intruded—empty beer cans being crushed, loud music, girls running around shrieking in the hallway, drunken boys sneering and lurching after them, guitars playing out of tune. To Loh the sounds were surreal, sometimes far away, sometimes startlingly close. He was soaked in sweat, his forehead was burning, and his lips were parched. Inside the blanket and sheet, he wore a tattered coat, but his chill was getting worse.

Around midnight four strangers who had dropped off their backpacks in the dormitory before going out on the town flung open the door, spilling raucous laughter inside. Two of them were girls. One of the young men nudged Loh with his bare foot. "Hey, would you mind staying out in the hall for a bit?" another one asked. The rest probably sipped their beers, sneered, and stared at the small figure wrapped in a blanket and sheet. A command disguised as a question, a shameless act by stupid fools targeting someone they saw as vulnerable. In the dark beneath his covers, how would Loh have felt?

When Loh didn't respond, one of them began peeling off the sheet and blanket. Loh resisted, but not for long—he was at least a handspan shorter than they were and weak and ill from severe fatigue.

Before long the blanket and sheet came off and Loh lay exposed. A roar of laughter. "Look here, a little kid." I can hardly suppress my anger as I imagine their drunken arrogance and their ridicule. "How old are you?" "Chinese?" "Japanese?" They dissected him as if he were laid out on a surgical table, stripped of personality, a living specimen for an experiment. "Hey, little boy, you're not allowed in places like this without an adult," one of them joked; the rest chuckled. The girls made scary faces as if teasing a child. Loh reached for his blanket and sheet, but one of the guys grabbed them first. "Out! Now!" But Loh didn't understand, and the two men had to drag him out to the hall. Thus was Loh removed from the hostel room he'd paid for with his last euros. Guests in the hallway glanced at him as he sank feebly to the floor, shivering from fever. He dragged himself to the end of the hall to the shared bathroom.

The bathroom—as always, the only space in this city that offered him shelter.

Now, as then, drunken guests are cackling, and the music is too loud. I sit on my dormitory bed and hate with a passion those who can find no other way to express their youth. Wasting their youth in futile excitement is one thing, but I feel only contempt for those who would show disrespect to a stranger who's been evicted from his rightful place just for the sake of indulgence. Ignoring his dignity, disregarding how sick a person is—this enrages me. I hear someone snooping around in the hallway, and eventually, the door opens and I see a white guy with a bottle of vodka. Our eyes meet. "Wanna drink?" I give him a cold stare and shake my head. He shrugs and closes the door softly. This is too much. I get up, open the door, and call him.

"Hey!"

The man slowly turns. He looks drunk. I run up and shove him in the chest. He's sturdy and doesn't budge. He merely looks down at me, stunned. I glare at him as hard as I can.

"What are you doing?" he yells.

"Why are you so rude?" I bark.

"What are you talking about?"

"You, I'm talking about you! And you! And you, and you there!"

I point at random intoxicated guests as my screaming builds to a crescendo. Those I point at and those I don't are equally puzzled.

"Don't you have eyes and ears? Someone was sick and lying down in a room all by himself! But no one knew, no one! And you kicked him out of that room!"

"What?"

"Is it okay to do that? Who said you could do that?!" I yell at the top of my lungs, then collapse to the floor and groan. The pain doesn't make sense, but it's welled up from deep inside and now it saturates me. Loh, Yunju, Jae—none of them can comfort me at this point. The pain comes from no one. It was three years ago. These people aren't the ones from back then. My mind understands this truth, but my heart evades it.

"She's hammered," people mutter under their breath. Am I really? I haven't had anything to drink today, so what is it that has roused me?

My unreasonable outburst has an unintended result.

"Are you okay?"

The question comes from an Asian woman I've never seen before and from the white man I shoved. They approach me and give me a pat on the shoulder, as if to comfort me. I look up to see who all is there, but I can't focus. Declining someone's helping hand, I get to my feet. The white guy is genuinely sorry, and yet for the life of me, I can't apologize to this person who has offered understanding rather than criticism or blame. I stagger among the guests who crowd the hallway, watching me with suspicion as I head toward the bathroom.

When I was young and had bad dreams, I would feel relieved that the gloomy world from which I'd awakened was just a dream. Though it wasn't real, I'd feel desolate nonetheless. Maybe because I knew the dream had some strange foothold in reality and that I would eventually return to that place where voice, sense, emotion, family, and relationships disappear. Those dreams have helped me to understand why I am desolate now. I know that the place I have to return to is not shared. It's not a space where one can mourn while others watch. Instead, it's a place of solitude removed from others' eyes—a space in which I have to question the very nature of the sadness I feel.

After being dragged from his room, Loh stayed perched on the toilet until early morning. At dawn he returned to his room, where the two men and two women were tangled in sleep. He quietly packed and, for the first time since checking in at the hostel, skipped breakfast. In his wallet, six euros and fifty-two cents remained in the waterproof wrapper. Since his trip to the embassy, he hadn't spent a cent on anything other than his room charges.

December 17, 2010. Friday

I pack and leave at 6 a.m. The short-haired woman in jeans has the early-morning shift and spends it dozing at the reception table. I set my suitcase down, approach slowly, and knock twice on the table with the back of my hand.

She jolts awake, looks up at me with fuzzy eyes, and immediately frowns. *You again.* Annoyance clouds her makeup-free face. I lean over the table and ask her in a deliberate voice, "Three years ago a short Asian man stayed here a bit over two weeks. Do you remember?"

"Look, this is a hostel. How many people do you think check in and out of here per day?"

"He used to put rolls and jam in his pockets at breakfast every morning."

"Impossible. It's prohibited."

"He wrote that he was never caught."

"He wrote what?"

"In any case, you're saying you don't remember. On his last day, he would have looked thin and sick. He had a severe cold, and he was very tired."

"Your story, when does it end?"

"Why didn't you treat him with a little kindness?"

"What?"

"If you ever see him again, please apologize to him—and be sincere."

"Are you in your right mind?"

"My story ends here."

As I turn toward my suitcase, I hear a grumbled retort. I don't know French curse words, but what she mumbles is hostile and crude. Brussels early in the morning is cold. It would have been colder three years ago when it rained.

Drenched without an umbrella, Loh walked to Cathédrale des Saints-Michel-et-Gudule. From Rue Neuve he turned left onto Rue du Persil, then onto Rue des Comédiens, and while on Rue du Bois Sauvage, he heard the church bells pealing in the early morning air. The reverberations penetrated through him, tempering his past woes, and echoed in the beating of his heart and the breaths he took. Loh had the extraordinary sensation of merging with the tolling of the bells, and he followed the sound the way a blind person might. It led him to a church and to the dark tranquility inside, where a scant few seniors populated the pews. I sit at the very back as Loh did that day. The church smells like my grandma, like a dying body resisting the end of life. Like the stink that assailed me whenever I had to enter a hospital intensive care unit for research and filming. Like the odor of a person wasting away in the limited time allotted the body.

The pipe organ starts playing.

Loh didn't believe in God and disliked the hubris of believers, but he prayed as the organ delivered its solemn, sorrowful tune. He prayed for his mother, whose deathbed he couldn't attend, whose body he failed to protect. Had he ever prayed before? I'm approaching the pages in Loh's journal where my breath always catches, passages I can't read through without pausing.

Even after the music stops, the tears Loh shed elude me. As before, I can't perfectly recreate someone else's experiences or emotions, and yet this inability also affords me relief. But why should I want to hide behind this relief? Three years ago, sitting where I am now, Loh was huddled up, shaking and sobbing. What relief is there in knowing

I can only imagine such a devastating moment? An absent hand searches my dry face in vain.

When I return to Pak's apartment from Cathédrale des Saints-Michel-et-Gudule and open the door, a pair of black shoes catches my eye. Pak's shoes. The unexpected visit is inconvenient but not unpleasant. I stay here temporarily, and Pak of course owns the place. I change into slippers, go into the kitchen, and there he is sitting at the dining table, as I thought. Dawn has blossomed, and the sun already peeks in, but the apartment remains dim without the lights on. I fumble for the light switch in the kitchen but Pak says don't. My hand in midair, I pause at the deep bass of his voice. He's been drinking wine. Since when? Last night? An empty wine bottle sits on the table.

"I was taking a walk and thought of you. I happened to have a spare key in my bag."

Making up stories is uncharacteristic of Pak. It's unlikely the visit is a coincidence. Either he carries a key at all times or he made a point of putting it in plain sight this morning or last night as he rehearsed what he wants to tell me, what he must tell me, and what he shouldn't tell me. I unwrap my scarf, remove my coat, place it over the back of a chair, and sit down across from him.

"I brought something."

He takes out a photograph—one more "coincidence"—from his bag on the floor and hands it to me. It's a photo of Loh. Taken when he was staying at Foyer Selah, Pak says. Carefully holding the photo, I gaze into it. Not so different from what I imagined: a youthful face, thick bushy hair, bony cheeks, a worn winter coat, clear black eyes that harbor a hint of worry. What my imagination misconstrued is his smile and the innocence of his face. His expression alone gives me great comfort. A sturdy dark-skinned woman has an arm around his shoulder. She must be Sylvie, the Foyer Selah staffer who wrote "Knocking on Heaven's Door" on a Post-it note for him.

"How is your writing coming along?"

I offer a leisurely shake of the head in response. Since writing that first sentence, "In the beginning he was just an initial, L.," I've managed to produce a few lines every day, but I'm not happy with it. I once told Jae that whether I was working on a script or something else, my goal was to portray a subject's invisible tears with deep compassion. Visualizing Loh's tears as I read his journal often saddens me, but I'm still not sure of myself. As I trace his path, I discover that he and I are alike, but rather than empathizing deeply with his grief, I observe from afar and put more effort into justifying my past decisions. I'm not yet convinced that I deserve the task I've set for myself.

"Would you like a glass of wine?" asks Pak. I nod and slip the photograph among the pages of Loh's journal in my bag.

Pak gets up and crosses the kitchen. In a cabinet I haven't opened yet are glasses and wine bottles in neat rows. It strikes me that for Pak the cabinet is like a box of candies, what my pillbox has been for me. But instead of sweets, Pak's box dispenses temporary amnesia and a promise to share the pain. Pak broods over the array of wines before returning with a bottle and a glass. He has to wrestle the cork free, but his hands show a familiarity with corkscrews that's acquired through repetition.

"You must like wine."

"It's better than sleeping pills."

"Do you have trouble sleeping?"

"Can't avoid it when you're old like me," Pak says as he carefully pours wine for both of us. "It's Spanish," he explains. "People fuss about French wine being good, Chilean better, and Italian the best, but for me Spanish wine is the real thing. Cheers."

I don't enjoy wine and know nothing of labels or regional differences in taste. But just now I really want to drink. When one wants to flee a lucid mind, prolonged tension, or angst, alcohol works as well as sleeping pills.

"Tell me," I begin in a tired voice after my first sip. Pak gazes at me from across the table. "You didn't come here just to give me that picture. You have something to tell me?"

"You're tactful all right. But it doesn't have to be you in particular."

"Then loosen up and tell me, if it doesn't matter who listens."

"It's been five years, but the memory sometimes returns like it was yesterday. On those nights I can't sleep a wink."

Pak wants to tell me something from five years ago. He already told me on our last stroll that without anyone knowing, he'd helped a patient with liver cancer die peacefully and immediately afterward closed down his practice.

"You mean the patient with end-stage liver cancer."

"You have a good memory."

"It made an impression."

"I can imagine."

I quickly drain the glass. Coming after a day of starvation and fatigue, it relaxes my body in no time, even turns Pak a bit blurry. He downs two more glasses, and I pour him another. His temples have reddened somewhat by the time he speaks again.

"I used a barbiturate. Dignitas, the well-known Swiss organization for euthanasia, uses it. I know in theory how it slows breathing through chemical reactions, but I can't know from experience how much confusion or pain it causes the patient."

"Less pain than if you died in a fire."

"Are you so certain?"

I don't know how to respond. Pak continues after a pause.

"Here is a patient with end-stage liver cancer. Let's say fluid builds up in the abdomen, and hepatic encephalopathy is imminent. Once that happens, she won't recognize her face in the mirror. She'll lose bowel control, so the body will stink. We can up the painkiller dosage, but the day soon comes when even morphine stops working. And so the patient wails in pain like a beast until suffering itself knocks her out. She may develop bedsores from lying all day connected to pipes and tubes." Pak turns to me. "Do you understand what I'm saying? Her soul, her sublime life, erodes away within the prison of this viciously ravaged body. Pain overwhelms everything."

He pauses again, then asks, "Does dying require such a process? Here was a woman of dignity and resolve, who always kept her struggles private and presented a strong front to others, even her own family. Is it right to witness the utter destruction of someone so tidy and neat?"

"I—"

"That's okay," says Pak, as he gets to his feet. "It's no use." I doubt he expected a response or wanted to know my thoughts. He just wanted to talk. To confess about the most profound moment in his life and be assured by a total stranger that what happened was justified. Perhaps he also sought some reckoning for his own continued good health. When I first met Pak, I had the impression he didn't indulge his emotions and that he'd long been injury-free. I wonder now if I was mistaken.

Pak goes to the window and quietly watches the early morning streets stir to life. But looking closer I realize he's actually gazing into his own past. His back is stooped, a posture that yearns, beyond anything I've seen, for warmth from someone. I know this look. Before I know it, I'm walking toward the window. As I do Pak turns, and a question I've been burning to ask him—to ask anyone—stops at the tip of my tongue. It's only ten steps from the dining table to the window, but in that moment Pak's soul is far away: steps by themselves, no matter how many, cannot take me to him.

As on any other day, Loh's mother had received a call and went after supper to work at the karaoke bar. She never returned. That was September 11, 2007. Loh paced and chain-smoked in front of their house until the wee hours, then fell asleep. Around eight in the morning, an urgent hand shook him awake. When he saw that the hand belonged to his mother's uncle, Loh knew something terrible had happened, though he didn't yet know, or in that moment want to know, just how terrible. But inexorably, the news unfolded, and no amount of shock or disbelief could keep his perfect, merciless ears from hearing it.

Leaving work at midnight, Loh's mother had been struck by a car and died soon after at a local hospital. Loh asked and then begged to be taken there, then fell to the floor and pleaded at least for the name of the hospital. But telling him any of this was too risky: the Chinese government already hunted for North Korean defectors and offered the police lump-sum awards for their capture. A police camp had quickly materialized near the hospital once they learned where Loh's mother was from. Even hearing Loh wail, his great uncle knew that Loh's mom, now dead at just forty-two, would have wanted Loh protected in this way.

A clock ticked indifferently in the silence.

Two days later Loh's relative visited again, this time with two missionaries from South Korea. Loh hadn't eaten in the interim and looked emaciated. Thoughts of suicide had darkened his eyes. Between feeling he didn't deserve such suffering and his refusal to face the loss, he'd come close to the brink. And yet somehow he persevered through the hopelessness and escaped the abyss. For his part, Loh's relative offered the comfort of a specific directive: go to Europe—and, oddly, the South Korean missionaries, who before had urged him toward South Korea, agreed. The European countries, they said, had good welfare systems and opportunities that drew refugees from across the world. And then one of them made an appalling suggestion: there was a market for dead bodies. With the proceeds Loh wouldn't have to worry about the expense of resettling in Europe. And the alternative? If no one else retrieved the body, the Chinese government would take custody, meaning it would simply disappear. At first Loh couldn't even process the idea and wondered, just for a moment, if this whole episode was a lie or a trick. But his relative finally made him see: "Your survival is the way to keep your mother's will alive." Loh was too drained to cry.

Four thousand US dollars reached Loh within a week. He went to the Korean church his mother used to attend and shivered for no apparent reason as he waited for the missionaries to arrive. When they did, Loh tithed and entrusted them with his mother's memorial service. The broker charged $2,800 for plane tickets and a forged South Korean passport. Loh had to spend some more on luggage, a pair of comfortable shoes, a scarf, and a pair of gloves. The rest, including a sum given by his relative, amounted to 650 euros after exchange. Loh found a piece of waterproof fabric and wrapped the bills securely. *I will protect it from rain, sweat, and tears. Neither falling rocks nor thunderclouds will hurt it.* Loh didn't unwrap the package even once until he was en route to Berlin.

Loh must have known that releasing his mother's body would redefine his life, that the ensuing regret and bone-melting agony were permanent. The remorse would resurface, each time more profoundly than the last. No matter how far he ran through time, each glance backward would relitigate his choice and demand self-contempt. I want to know where along that path Loh stands at this moment.

And likewise for Yunju. I'm anxious to know her thoughts when she looks in a mirror and sees the lump, which had first brought shame and anger and then threatened her life. How is Yunju dealing with a tumor composed of her own hurtful tears and the reckless stares of strangers whose poisons then distilled into a malignant cancer? Does she accept it at all?

I can know none of this with certainty, of course. One doesn't own or really know the pains of others—one can only guess. I've always been ignorant, powerless to help, and late to arrive when someone needs me the most. I had long decided I could never know exactly where another person's suffering starts, when it peaks, how it proceeds, how it infiltrates the person's life, and how it occupies his or her waking hours. Perhaps it was this habitual noncommitment that led Loh's words to jar me so badly, call so deeply into question where I stood. After recounting an arduous journey bereft of comfort or warmth and clouded with fatigue, Loh told the reporter, "I traded my mother for my own survival. That's why I had to live."

~

As he turns from the window, I ask Pak if he understands Loh's words. When he doesn't immediately answer, I ask if empathy with Loh's guilt over his mother inspired Pak to help him. Pak is now so close I can hear him breathing. No answer this time, either. Instead, he asks if it was that sentence from the article that led me here. I nod, adding that I don't know how to carry on living when, thanks to my mistake, someone is now either dead or so unhappy she may as well be. Pak cocks his head in thought, then asks if one person's death or unhappiness is ever someone else's fault. Too abruptly, I say that maybe the question voices his own guilt over killing that end-stage cancer patient five years ago.

"No," he replies, "you're wrong. Euthanasia is not simply the act of injecting a fatal drug. That decision is ultimately the patient's—doctors may do nothing without the patient's permission. In my case, I chose to place a mixture of the drug and alcohol in the patient's room. As a doctor, I was not allowed to be party to the patient's decision whether to drink the cocktail. So I wasn't."

"But because you brought the cup to her, she could execute her choice."

"Nothing is more decisive than the will of a person who chooses to die."

"Are there no miracles in this world? Didn't your involvement rob her of that possibility?"

Pak gapes at me, as if speechless. I hold his gaze.

"You think I killed the patient."

"You swapped her dignity for her life, I'd say."

"What do you want me to say?"

"I just want to ask. Those who remain, the healthy ones: What should they do, other than constantly justify their own existence with excuses? How should they feel toward those who have died or become so unhappy they want to? Do you have an answer for that?"

Pak turns pale and glares at me. I tremble slightly. A tragic circumstance and a sincere request for euthanasia from the patient are necessary conditions for a doctor to act, but they don't require him to do so. Pak suffers because he knows this.

He wasn't able to share the patient's suffering at the threshold of death—an impossibility anyway. Even so, Pak is afflicted with insomnia. His bearing—the ashen face, the resolutely closed mouth that looks like it will never open again, the rapid pulse that has him quivering all over—reveals his inner turmoil. What am I, then? What do I expect by cornering him into exhausting introspection and excruciating repentance? Am I saying that he and I are accomplices in life, that we cannot and should not be forgiven?

"You two are alike," he says finally. Seeing my quizzical look, he adds, "The patient and you, Kim *chakka*. Neither of you allows yourself an inch of generosity. I felt that the first time I saw you."

"That patient . . . she wasn't just a patient to you, was she?"

My words, devoid of generosity, confirm his diagnosis. His eyes widen at this last question. When I maintain his gaze, Pak turns away, and a dense, intolerable stillness settles over the two of us. A long while later, Pak declares he's leaving. I don't object—I won't corner him forever. He passes by me, showing no effects from the wine. He won't contact me for a while. Once again I've lost an opportunity to ask him how one decides, as Loh did, that survival is a duty. It waits for another day to explain that my motive in coming here to learn about Loh's life was to accept that I, too, must live.

December 18, 2010. Saturday

The words "malicious" and "regret," in the voice of Yunju's surgeon, reverberate through my nightmare as I wake. It's 2 p.m.—10 p.m. in Korea. As if by instinct, I turn off my cell phone. Switching off a phone won't turn off my memory, but it's all I can do. My scribbles remain too, of course—in my notepad, on the back of a receipt in my wallet, on a page in the guidebook I carry everywhere, on the margins of a map of Brussels.

Today is Yunju's operation.

A moment later I slide off the sofa onto my knees, turn on my phone again, and dial Jae's number. Every pore of my body exudes a sense of dread.

Jae picks up on the first ring. I'm in a sweat as he tells me Yunju had the surgery as scheduled this morning. I hold my breath, waiting for news of its success. He states matter-of-factly that the chemotherapy was effective, that the metastasis has been stopped, and that the surgery was therefore uneventful. With Yunju's consent they filmed the procedure; the show will air in a month. My wrist, numb from gripping the phone so tightly, begins to relax.

"But," he continues, and I realize how heavy and dark his voice has been. "But they couldn't save her right ear."

"What do you mean?"

"The cancer spread, and they had to remove it."

I ponder this unexpected outcome. While my perfectly healthy body wallowed in baseless and self-indulgent misery, Yunju confronted a genuine threat, a lump that first disfigured her and then cost her an ear. "Yunju must be devastated," I muse.

"Not yet," says Jae. "She's still wrapped in bandages."

"Jae—" It's been ages since I called him by name. "Yes?" he answers.

My mind whirls with things I want to say to him, things I must tell him, and words I mustn't speak. "I . . . it's like before. I learned too late, again."

The line is silent—perhaps Jae is pondering my words? What would it be like for a girl, not quite eighteen, to lose an ear? I want to ask Jae if I, in good health and with two matching ears, am allowed to confess my own pain and say it's real.

Jae stays silent. Without another word I flip the phone closed and lie back again on the sofa, where I remain the rest of the day, fighting the onset of a cold. Sometime during this stretch, Yunju's lost ear crept into my imaginings. *It* nested itself under the sofa and watched me through the day until nighttime. When I briefly opened my eyes in the middle of the night, *It* made its way into my heart and measured its temperature.

December 20, 2010. Monday

I don't know real starvation. Poverty for me was always relative, a sense of lack based on imagining life for those with more. Jae seemed genuinely sympathetic when I told him that in college I couldn't afford any of the class outings or spend summers volunteering on a farm; even working several tutoring jobs, I barely made tuition. But I have no grasp of deep hunger—the kind that makes you hallucinate, beg on the street, rummage through trash, or fall down from weakness. I don't know anyone who does.

Loh exited the cathedral and continued on his way. December 20 fell on a Thursday that year. Brussels in the week before Christmas is vibrant and spectacular, but to Loh, who grew up in an impoverished country in East Asia, the jaunty footsteps and abundant laughter felt vain. His sickness had dug in, and hunger grew sharper every day. His pockets held no more rolls. That night he found a discarded sandwich in a roadside dumpster, ate it, walked into Gare du Midi and fell asleep on a bench. The station had no heat, so it was no warmer than lying down on the street. But even this refuge was not to be. Despite his now running a fever, neither the station attendants nor the homeless regulars who'd already marked off their territories had any intention of taking in this diminutive new arrival from Asia. They evicted him at 2 a.m. He proceeded to the restroom in the underground passageway connecting the train and subway stations. The facility had an automatic lock operated by a fifty-cent coin. Loh paid it, entered the innermost stall as usual, crouched on the toilet with his coat zipped all the way up and his head wrapped in a scarf, and slept. Once in a while, he would jolt awake and fumble for the waterproof fabric package containing his remaining six euros and two cents.

Loh slept in the same stall the next night too. Five euros and fifty-two cents.

December 22, 2007, the Saturday before Christmas, was festive indeed. It also marked Loh's third day of homelessness, his third day without food, and his first moment as a beggar. In the Trone subway station, at the foot of the stairs leading toward Arts-Loi, Loh took off his hat, knelt down, bent at the waist, and placed the hat in front of him, so claiming his place among the basest inhabitants of the world. Each of those movements replays in slow motion in my head. My brain rejects cheap pity, but I can't help lamenting as this excruciating scene plays out. His preparations complete, Loh took a harmonica from his bag and began to play. He soon lost count of how many tunes he played or how many hours he spent there. In all he gathered about five euros.

No one is begging at the Arts-Loi staircase today. I try to imagine where Loh positioned himself, then sit in that spot. As I shiver with cold, people rushing by glance at me. Soon a fit of coughing forces me back to my feet. I head on toward Place de la Bourse.

With ten euros in hand, Loh walked on, semiconscious with fatigue despite having napped fitfully between sets with his harmonica. Was it a simple desire to eat, or a defiant determination to walk until the end, that drove him? He stopped at Place de la Bourse, which featured a cluster of Asian restaurants, including Chinese, Indian, Thai, and Vietnamese. It was at this intersection that Loh saw red moths. *Beautiful,* he would have whispered to himself. His journal records how, when he saw the splendor of the city lights in Brussels, he imagined nocturnal moths of all sizes coming awake at dusk, turning lights on in their bodies, and flying through the city. The streets of Brussels must have been desperately beautiful that night.

Mesmerized, Loh followed the red moths—so close he could almost touch them—first one, then dozens, then beyond counting, as thick as Christmas lights in the trees. He imagined them leading him home. Maybe his mother would come out to greet him. The smell of food grew thicker, and his steps hastened.

At the entrance to Place de la Bourse, I look up at the red lights, blink, and then stare in disbelief as a huge flurry of moths take wing. I reach my arm into the brilliant cascade, and my hair and body glow bright red.

As if in thrall, I walk along the row of trees, letting the lights guide me as they had Loh. The smaller trees lead to a tall spruce in their midst, decorated as a Christmas tree. Although his pocket now contained a few bills, soaked through with feverish sweat, Loh didn't seek out a restaurant. Instead, he sat down on a bench under this tree and surrendered to fatigue. His entire body relaxed, then ebbed into unconsciousness.

Perhaps he intended to give in that night. He was too tired to resume his journey, which had no destination in the first place. Maybe he came to this spot following a whim, having decided that if he was to fade, at least it could be in a place full of red moths and the smell of food.

The next morning he woke up in a police station.

December 21, 2010. Tuesday

Loh opened his eyes to find himself on a sofa near a busy entrance and soon realized where he was. Men in winter coats with "Police" stenciled on the back hurried to and fro, and loud voices sounded throughout the station. Anyone of illegal status would have avoided such a place, but Loh, carried here unconscious, had no say in the matter. Seeing him wake, a middle-aged policeman approached with a file in hand and asked him a few questions. Name, address, family, and nationality, Loh guessed, but he had no answers: he'd lost all of these except his name, and in any case he couldn't have answered with simple hand gestures. He thought for a moment of showing the forged South Korean passport in his bag but immediately dismissed the idea. A document sure to be revealed as fake would only justify suspicion, not prove his identity. So Loh kept silent and evaded the officer's discerning eyes.

That afternoon, the day before Christmas Eve, Loh was taken by police car to an orphanage in a suburb of Brussels. He would have been anxious and wanted to ask where they were going. Or maybe his questions were more fundamental: Why am I here in Brussels? How did I manage to come so far from home? Is this where I'll spend the rest of my life?

Seeing the new Asian guest arrive in a police car, the children at the orphanage would have wondered about Loh's age or where he was from.

Their suspicious eyes on his back, Loh and the officer went inside and down the hallway to the office, where they met Ellen, the director. She was the first person in Brussels to offer Loh real help. The officer introduced him as a vagrant. Loh learned of this mistake sometime later, after he left Foyer Selah to work at a Chinese restaurant on Rue Rasson. Loh liked to visit Ellen at the orphanage on payday. "Didn't the officer say he thought I was mute or mentally ill?" he would joke to her in weak but grammatical French. This amusing reminiscence is recorded toward the very end of his journal. But a year earlier, on that afternoon before Christmas Eve, he was unable to explain that he was a twenty-year-old adult and not a boy in his early teens.

Loh, assumed to be thirteen or fourteen, was assigned a room in a building housing boys and girls aged ten to fourteen. Depositing his bag there, Loh followed Ellen's directions and took a long shower, changed into jeans and a shirt provided by the orphanage, and went to the cafeteria.

Dinner that night was festive. Seated before a full holiday spread and not just soup and bread, Loh temporarily forgot his woes and the uprooting that had caused them. He'd eaten nothing for four days, but in truth this was his first square meal since arriving in Brussels. Other orphans, wounded by their own abandonment and acutely frigid toward a stranger, glared as Loh gobbled bread and meat in a daze. Loh was too starved to let those eyes affect him, and besides, they were just kids. Loh chewed, swallowed, and drank nonstop until his plate was empty.

That night a scuffle broke out. The boys and girls were upset with this person who'd entered their world without permission and ate like an animal in their midst. Driven by their collective broken hearts, they ganged up on Loh, wrapped him in comforters and blankets, and took turns punching and kicking him. There were other voices telling the assailants to stop, but Loh wouldn't have understood the foreign words. Suffering alone under his blankets, would he have recalled that other night in the dormitory room at Good Sleep Hostel? Or his first night in Brussels, when smoking in his room provoked a threat? Would he have silently validated his prediction that disrespect, contempt, wariness, and needless misunderstandings would define his life in this city?

Loh endured the hostility, pretending that he, like them, was just another abandoned youth. Bruises on his back, bloodied lips, a broken arm, and being knocked senseless were nothing to him. But soon he embraced this overdue retribution for selling his mother's body so he could flee to Europe and save his own skin. The South Korean missionaries had romanticized his act as sublime, while the ticket broker and his charges, who boarded the plane to Berlin with Loh, could not have cared less about his story. Loh wanted someone, anyone, to recognize the monster he was and punish him. It made no difference if the punishment came at the hands of teenagers. *Go ahead and kill me,* Loh might have whispered from inside the blankets. *Hit me harder. Please.* When Loh put up no fight, the violence eased. The attackers, sated for now, returned to their assigned beds and their childlike thoughts of presents and a Santa Claus who could save them in real life. Christmas was around the corner, and they knew that for some of them, their fate would soon change.

When all was still, Loh emerged from his blankets and walked to the shared shower at the end of the hall, where he stanched the bleeding and tried to conceal the bruises behind hair or clothing. He didn't want to provoke an uproar by exposing wrongful violence. At least here at the orphanage, he didn't need to roam the streets shivering with cold, begging for food, and looking down at the ground in hunger. Loh figured, correctly, that the beatings would continue for at least a week.

Walking near the orphanage, I think about a twenty-year-old Loh, taken for a child and subject to neglect and group assaults for some fifteen days. But soon my attention wanders, so I reach into my pocket and take out the little Christmas card that Ellen just handed me, saying to pass it along to Loh when I meet him. Her card makes me feel that Christmas is near.

I take out my cell phone, which hasn't rung since my short conversation with Jae three days ago.

As if compelled, I slowly enter Yunju's number. We might start with banal words, like noting that it's Christmas. *That's right,* the other would affirm. *Can you imagine a twenty-year-old man in an orphanage, eating free food and trying to fit in among children singing Christmas carols?* I'd ask then. *Well, not really,* she might reply, looking out the hospital window with a sheepish smile. And if she were to ask how he ended up in an orphanage, I'd like to tell her: *He must have been lonely, like you.*

Yunju doesn't answer. Perhaps she's looking in a mirror, a flawed one that can't show her right ear or display happiness, whose only image is a wretched seventeen-year-old, cold and sorrowful as winter.

Loh departed the orphanage sooner than expected. One day Ellen came upon him among the kitchen staff, singing while doing dishes. A decade ago she'd worked briefly connecting Korean adoption agencies with Belgian adoptive parents and remembered a smattering of the language. After bringing him to her office, she regarded him for a moment with humane eyes. "Coréen?" she asked. Loh sensed a moment for honesty, besides which there was nowhere to run or hide. Loh got up from his chair, removed the knit hat given him by the orphanage, and bowed politely. *Korean,* he nodded. Ellen pointed up and down: *North or South?*

North, he repeated her gesture. *North Korea.*

Loh's answer, both word and gesture, would have been decisive and clear. The words "North Korea" and "DPRK," English names for his home country, occur on the first page of his journal and repeatedly throughout. This repeated effort to write them down showed a need to speak his own nationality, a core identity from which he'd been cut loose. When Ellen nodded that she understood, Loh gained confidence and used his hands to say he was twenty years old. Ellen was stunned. Tellingly, instead of asking if that was his real age, she called the South Korean embassy, grew frustrated by their half-hearted response, then called the Belgian Ministry of the Interior. Ministry staff visited the orphanage two days later.

The name of the song Loh sang while doing dishes is not recorded in his journal.

I return to Pak's apartment, shower, settle on the sofa, and take out my cell phone. It's been three days since I spoke to Jae. He picks up on the third ring. I want to ask about Yunju after she gained consciousness, but I can't even utter the name. Thankfully, Jae mentions it first and says she's mending gradually. "Yunju . . ." This time I say the name. I want to ask if she blames me still but I can't. Instead, I tell him I'm lonely. He says he understands. When I stay silent, he asks how goes my writing. "In bits and pieces," I tell him. He whispers that he's relieved. I want to say I miss him, but the words don't come, and what I do say after a long pause betrays me. I may have said I was sorry. He doesn't respond at first, then says he still hasn't filled my position as lead writer. Not something I wanted to hear. The gap between us reasserts itself, and soon we hang up. My phone informs me that our conversation lasted one minute and fifty-two seconds.

I find my box of pills and, like before, close my eyes and rummage through to pick one out at random. A sleeping pill, again. After downing it with water, I retrace the short conversation with Jae until my consciousness blurs, until only the apology, persistent and troubling, stands between me and sleep. I can't be responsible for that innermost part of my heart that speaks its own truth and blurts out that I'm sorry. The thoughts push back against the effects of the five-hundred-milligram pill and make me restless. I lay myself down on the sofa, then sit on the living-room floor, then stand again and go lean against the window.

The same *It* that gauged the temperature of my heart four days ago reappears in silhouette and starts singing by my ear. Lulled by the song, I finally fall asleep around two in the morning.

~

With the help of ministry staff, Loh submitted an application for refugee status at the Office of Alien Affairs within the ministry. After being photographed, fingerprinted, and subjected to a simple health check, he was granted temporary housing in an asylum in Waluwe-Saint-Pierre, a municipality of Brussels. Four days later he was summoned for interviews with Alien Affairs.

Loh met Pak for the first time at an interrogation by the division for refugee applications. The first session, attended by Pak and two ministry officers, took place at 10 a.m. on Friday, January 11, 2008. Through Pak as interpreter, the officers asked their questions and Loh answered. But Pak was more than just an interpreter: based on his knowledge of North Korea, he assessed Loh's accent, vocabulary, and familiarity with the country. Although it fell to ministry officers to pronounce Loh's story true or not, that assessment would depend heavily on Pak's sense of what was credible and accurate.

European countries in general are reluctant to grant refugee status to aliens who either deserted a country or were deported. No country in the world welcomes refugees unconditionally: granting status involves providing support for resettlement, and this requires money. In practice, this meant officers did their best to deny Loh's refugee status and deport him from Belgium, while Loh's best chances lay in being as honest as he could be. Pak remained objective by translating faithfully between the two sides. Neither Pak nor Loh could have predicted that this initial wary meeting would soon grow into a friendship or that each would become a mirror for the other, bringing to light things each had tried to hide.

Routine questions and answers dominated the first interview: name, age, hometown, family members, the local landscape, and life growing up. After several exchanges one of the officials placed a sheet of paper on the table, and Pak told Loh to draw his national flag. Loh's reproduction was meticulous, down to the red and blue colors. The official filed the drawing and Pak continued: "Sing your national anthem from start to finish." Loh rose, stood at attention, and sang. His journal that night notes that Pak listened to the verses with closed eyes.

Loh's interrogators then left him alone to write an essay describing his life, with special attention to how he ended up coming to Europe. A copy of this five-page essay, which begins "My name is Loh Kiwan, and I was born on May 18, 1987, in Ward 7, Seseon Village, Onsung County, North Hamkyung Province, Democratic People's Republic of Korea" and ends "I arrived in Brussels by bus on Friday, December 4, 2007" is now in my bag.

The second interview took place a week later. In the interim Pak translated Loh's essay into French and submitted copies to the South Korean embassy and related agencies. A week after the second interview, Pak and Loh met again, this time by themselves, at the asylum where Loh was staying. Pak told him that he'd enjoyed reading the essay. Then he turned somber and offered sincere condolences for the loss of Loh's mother. Brief pauses still punctuated the conversation that followed, but gone were the uncomfortable gazes where each side measured the other. Pak even smiled graciously, and seeing this, Loh realized that this meeting was private, not part of an official investigation. At the end Pak said, "I'll try to get a good result." Loh describes grinning at this. Was he still wearing that smile, his first since arriving in Brussels, as he recorded this episode in his journal? I hope so.

After this third meeting with Pak, Loh wrote that he thought often about his father, who died in a mining accident when Loh was five. Those reminiscences may be why, about two years later as he left for England, Loh sent Pak his journal chronicling his life in Brussels. Pak had helped him acquire refugee status, and Loh would have wanted to explain why he had to leave without saying good-bye. The journal would convey what couldn't be said over the phone.

Added to the last page of Loh's essay is this comment by Pak to the South Korean ambassador to Belgium:

Je vous envoie le texte de Loh Kiwan traduit en français. Bien qu'il ne dispose pas de pièce d'identité de la Corée du Nord, je suis sûr qu'il est Nord-Coréen. Je pense que lui tendre une main secourable est notre mission aujourd'hui. C'est une vérité à laquelle nous ne pouvons échapper. Nous devrions donc l'aider davantage autant au niveau humain et affectif qu'au niveau politique et administrative. Nous laissons submerger par les problèmes politiques jusqu'à oublier les souffrances individuelles, souvenez-vous s'il vous plait que ceci est notre tragédie. N'hésitez pas à me contacter en cas de doute ou pour une explication quelconque. Je vous prie d'agréer l'expression de mes sincere salutations.

I send you the text by Loh Kiwan translated into French. Although he has no identification from North Korea, I'm sure he is North Korean. I believe that offering him a helping hand is our mission today. It is a truth we can't escape. And we should help him more for human and subjective reasons than for political and administrative ones. We allow ourselves to be overwhelmed by political problems to the point that we forget the suffering of individuals; please remember that this is our tragedy. Do not hesitate to contact me in case of doubt or for further explanation. Please accept my sincere good wishes.

December 22, 2010. Wednesday

Arriving at the last twenty pages or so of Loh's journal, I can finally smile. These pages begin with the Ministry of the Interior granting Loh a temporary residence permit, then recount his life until just before he left for England to join a Filipino woman named Layka. During this time Loh searched for hope, learned of love, and strove not to be lonely. Perhaps because this was a busy stretch for him, entries from this period are short and terse.

A month after Loh was transferred to the asylum in Waluwe-Saint-Pierre, it was decided that he probably was from North Korea, one of the countries internationally recognized as a region of crisis. Based on that verdict, he received a temporary residence permit, renewable monthly, and fifty euros a week for living expenses. He also gained access to free French classes. At that point he was transferred yet again, this time to Foyer Selah, a Salvation Army facility that allows outings and visits and offers a more stable life. He was to remain there while Alien Affairs investigated for possible criminal history and verified his testimony, after which it would either grant or refuse him refugee status. There was nothing further Loh could do to influence this decision, so all that remained was to wait.

On the day a police car took Loh to Foyer Selah, Pak went to visit. As with the previous visit, Pak was there not at the bidding of the police or the ministry but solely out of concern for Loh. Loh was bursting with thoughts and questions about his changing circumstances, and Pak addressed them all in patient detail.

Foyer Selah, a warm-beige brick building, is located at 23 Boulevard d'Ypres, about a fifteen-minute walk from the Yser subway station. The area houses many Muslim immigrants, which may explain the abundance of darker complexions among those staffing the grocery stores on the street.

At the entrance to Foyer Selah, a few black men and a middle-aged woman who looks Latina laugh cheerfully as they share a smoke. They must be among the lucky foreigners whose applications for refugee status have been accepted and who now await the result. Foyer Selah is open to everyone, so I can just walk in.

Loh spent six months here, which included his first spring and summer in Brussels and his twenty-first birthday. Three times a week, he attended night classes in French at a nearby public school and reminisced about home while listening to music that Sylvie, one of the staffers, put on. Sometimes Loh toured the city with fellow residents. He even rode a Ferris wheel for the first time at an amusement park that opens every other month. Just imagining Loh's eyes taking in the city of Brussels from atop the Ferris wheel, and how they must have shone with earnest curiosity, lifts my spirits.

In his sixth month at Foyer Selah, Loh received notice from the Ministry of the Interior granting him refugee status. Given that investigations usually took a year or two, sometimes as many as ten, and how often they ended in rejection, Loh's case was exceptional. Pak's unequivocal support had surely helped; how fortunate that this person, only the second Loh had met in Brussels, turned out to be his benefactor! With his new status, Loh left Foyer Selah, found himself an apartment, and in accordance with Belgian law began receiving seven hundred euros for basic living expenses. This support and the free French classes continued until Loh found lawful employment at a Chinese restaurant.

In the office at Foyer Selah, Sylvie is seated at a desk by the window, immersed in her work as usual. I know it's her from the photograph Pak showed me. When I mention Loh's name, she rises halfway and asks in

English how I know him. I explain that I'm writing about him but am not a relative. I can see in her manner that Sylvie would have been kind and helpful in any case, as she was three years earlier when she responded to Loh by writing down the names of the song and singer. Meeting Sylvie now, it's clear that being considerate and attentive are reflexes with her.

I sit on the sofa, drink the coffee Sylvie has offered, and learn more about Loh. As she recalls it, about a month into his stay at Foyer Selah he offered to help with domestic duties such as cleaning, washing dishes, and laundry, for which they paid him five euros a week. The work wasn't demanding, but few of the residents were willing to spend their time earning so little at a place where everything came free. On top of that, they received regular living support. It was probably not the money Loh desired but rather the hard rigors of manual labor. Sylvie describes the silent dignity with which Loh took up each task. No wonder: with each measure of work, he'd have remembered his mother arriving back home in the wee hours, her legs swollen and her voice hoarse. Recalling as well his own helplessness at the time and how his mother alone worked to protect and hide him, his gift to her now was unflagging diligence in everything he did. "If told to sweep the stairs," Sylvie continues, "Loh would clean the nooks and crannies between the floorboards and wipe down the staircase windows. Tasked with dishes after supper, he'd close the door to the cafeteria only after washing every dish on the shelves and in the cabinets."

Each description made the portrait more robust. Given a mop to clean the hallway, he'd go at it until the whole floor shined—not just the hallway but also individual rooms and offices. The clothes he washed would be spotless, and if you handed him a cleaning pad, ancient scum on the appliances would finally vanish. No one worked harder, Sylvie recalls with affection. Of course, he applied the same diligence to languages, with the result that he learned French quicker than anyone else. As we conclude, she asks me to say hello for her if I meet him. I wonder if someone like me deserves such a meeting, but I keep the musing to myself.

Sylvie walks me to the front door. As I leave, I turn around several times to etch her face in my memory, and each time I do, she's still standing by the door, waving. Oh yes, if I do meet Loh, I'll definitely tell him the beautiful Sylvie asked about him. I'll do so amid light-hearted chatter about nothing in particular while I brush dust from his coat.

And of course I'll say hello for Pak as well. Loh will be most eager for news of he who had visited Loh weekly at Foyer Selah. He always came with a bag full of groceries. Pak was obliged to report to Alien Affairs about Loh's livelihood, but the visits answered a much deeper calling.

The relationship between Loh and Pak continued after Loh left Foyer Selah, took a job at a Chinese restaurant, and moved into a rental apartment with Chinese, Vietnamese, and Pakistani roommates. Pak no longer had to report on Loh but continued visiting anyway. Perhaps Pak's affinity for Loh expressed his remorse over a woman central to his own life. Loh felt guilt over his mother's death, and Pak, who chose to help his wife die, could appreciate that guilt keenly.

Pak knew that Loh had learned enough French to read and understand documents on his own, but he nonetheless enjoyed picking them one by one from the pile of Loh's mail and translating them into Korean. As at Foyer Selah, he would sit quietly and watch Loh eat the food he'd brought while it was still warm. Then Pak would present Loh with more language-learning materials and dictionaries. To what extent did Loh understand Pak's ministrations? Could he sense the piercing guilt behind Pak's kindness and consideration? For his part, Pak wouldn't have disclosed the source of his insight into Loh's failure to protect his mother. Perhaps Loh was just happy to see Pak, who reminded him not only of a father whose face he no longer remembered but also of his mother, who'd always put a spoon in his hand first no matter how little food they had. Pak anticipated these visits in equal measure. For both of them, camaraderie and cozy evenings belied an unspoken mutual recognition of the suffering each had endured. In contemplating all this, I lament with all my heart having cornered Pak the other day.

I sensed it was his wife whom Pak had given the lethal cocktail. But when did I become aware?

Evening, December 22, 2010. Wednesday

Loh and Layka.

I'm thinking about them now. They met for the first time in February 2009 at the Chinese restaurant on Rue Rasson, the journal notes. At that time Loh, twenty-two, had just obtained refugee status, while Layka, twenty-one, worked illegally on an expired tourist visa. In several places the journal also says, "Today I taught Layka French." But there's almost nothing about their personal lives—what brought the two of them together, what things they did, how they drew close, when they started to depend on each other, and which moment let them know they'd each found the one. What's clear is that being together attenuated both Loh's sense of loss in having nowhere to return to and Layka's unease that her illegal status might get exposed. Each of their moments together could only have confirmed the truth of their bond. They also wouldn't have been stingy or self-conscious about expressing it to each other. No longer solitary beings, they now inhabited a world of two, built on the optimism of their union. They'd walk among the citizens of Brussels, who towered over the two of them like the descendants of Titans. To them, however, the rest of the world dwindled into the background. Springtime itself seemed to tell Loh that never again would he suffer the piercing cold of December 2007. Even after closing Loh's journal, I can see the two of them, walking the streets of Brussels, heading as one into the distance until they vanish.

How did they start?

Perhaps simply, like Jae and me five years ago. Did one of them, too, chuckle silently at the inexplicable sensation their first meeting had provoked?

I was to have met Jae for the first time in a conference room at work. The broadcasting staff were supposed to gather there before heading out as a group to a nearby Japanese restaurant. But Jae didn't show at the conference room. The assessment proved wrong, but other staffers, accustomed to absent producers, assumed that Jae was lazy and eager for a professional title but not real work. After a round of introductions, we adjourned to the restaurant.

I drank more than usual that night but not more than the occasion called for. The coworkers I understood the least were those who got drunk and made a scene at work dinners or who passed out and had to be carried from the restaurant. How could they reveal that side of themselves while knowing they'd have to face everyone the next day and pretend it was business as usual? After downing a soju-beer "bomb," I left the dining area to use the restroom, figuring movement would reduce my tipsiness.

I thought I'd washed my face at the sink, but the only wetness I found when I left the restroom was on my blouse. *Must be tipsier than I thought.* My legs felt unsteady as I started back toward the main room. I even wondered if I should find someone's shoulder for support.

When I arrived back at the entrance to the dining room, I noticed a pair of dark-brown suede sneakers with shabby seams. Amid the scattering of other shoes, these were placed neatly as a pair facing away from the room. It was November, and a green leaf had fallen on top of one toe. Where had they trudged to find and gather a leaf so green? I squatted down and studied them in a way I wouldn't have done if stone-cold sober. The owner must know of a secret forest in this city, unknown to all others. Or maybe the shoes were here on their own, just arrived from a leisurely stroll through the hidden wood.

"What are you doing there, Kim *chakka?*"

One of my coworkers had just opened the sliding door to come out, and there I was, peering at shoes for all to see. A man I hadn't noticed before I left the room craned his head to see.

"Say hello, Kim *chakka.* This is Ryu Jae, our producer. He went to see the granny from the first episode. Granny Choe Okpun. She lives in Chongseon with her two blind granddaughters, remember?"

Thus introduced, we exchanged awkward bows.

Over a business dinner a year later, after we got to know each other through and beyond work, Jae reminisced about the moment. "How is it you were smiling like a fool?" he asked while searching the broadcasting company archive for program music. His face showed genuine curiosity and perhaps a hint of teasing as he continued. "Now that I think about it, you were sitting alone in front of shoes smiling to yourself. Did you find money or valuables there?"

I scratched my head and pretended I didn't remember, but I remembered like it was yesterday. As I sat across from Jae in my wet blouse, as we shared drinks and discussed my writing, as he left the room to take a phone call, and as he bent to put on his suede sneakers with the leaf on top—I knew I'd already given a piece of my heart. In my preoccupation, I didn't even notice whether the drink I'd just been poured was beer, soju, sake, or whiskey.

"Did some charming guy just ask you out, Kim *chakka?*" one of the lighting crew teased. Only then did I realize I'd been grinning the whole time.

December 23, 2010. Thursday

Loh's one and only apartment in Brussels, rented after he acquired refugee status and left Foyer Selah, is located at Rue de Naples near the Porte de Namur subway station. He lived there over a year.

A sharp metallic noise—perhaps from the shoe plates inside my worn soles—follows me down Rue de Naples in the tranquility of dusk. The area, occupied mainly by people of color, grows shabbier as I proceed. A few of the residents, leaning against the wall smoking, gesture and ask me for money or cigarettes.

I arrive in front of Loh's apartment, which looks more like a row house than an apartment building. Like most buildings on this street, colorful graffiti masks a scarcely painted outer wall. I must navigate through the garbage littering the entrance before I can browse the handwritten list of residents mounted inside a clear plastic panel. The name Loh Kiwan would have appeared on this list a year ago. Would Loh have written his name in hangul or in the Latin alphabet? What were his thoughts as he wrote his name? Did his face show emotion when he finally landed a room of his own and attached his name to it?

Loh's room was on the fourth floor. I don't know the floor size, but adding in three other roommates—from China, Vietnam, and Pakistan—would have meant tight quarters. The four of them together put up curtains to give each a bit of privacy. Returning at midnight from the Chinese restaurant, Loh would lift up his curtains to reach his spot, sit down on his bed to have a supper of leftovers from the restaurant, and then study French or English textbooks. The name of the restaurant was Jin Shan Hua, and Layka was a waitress there when Loh landed the job.

A hunched old man arrives and takes out a key. I hang around as if I'm visiting one of the residents, then slip into the building after he opens the front door. The interior is much darker and more humid than I expected. Poor ventilation leaves a dank smell, a lone light bulb flickers from the ceiling, and dusty wooden stairs screech the building's history when they bear a person's weight.

Layka was the first to leave for England. She'd been rounded up in a police crackdown on shops and restaurants employing illegal workers. The savvy owner of Jin Shan Hua presented a forged labor certificate for Layka and lied about not knowing she was illegal. The restaurant was fined, but the consequences for Layka were much worse: detention in a camp for illegal aliens followed by deportation. Miraculously, Layka escaped the camp after a month, and of course she ran through the streets of Brussels straight to this apartment. I imagine their despairing hug in front of this door and their intense gratitude for each other's presence. Although neither knew what tomorrow would bring, their lover's embrace knew no regrets.

A relative of Loh's Vietnamese roommate agreed to hide Layka temporarily. Meanwhile, Loh began discreetly searching for a truck driver bound for England. They chose England because, compared to other European countries, it was generous to illegal immigrants, jobs were easier to find, and Layka could speak the language. But getting there would be difficult for an illegal alien without valid identification. Knowing that a truck's cargo area was a common means of smuggling illegal immigrants, police were stationed at the mouth of the Eurotunnel connecting England and the Continent. Carelessness in the midst of regular freight could lead to injury or, in rare cases, death. Once caught, the alien was subject by law to immediate deportation and prohibition from reentry into any European Union country for five years. But Loh and Layka had no other option. When one's very existence runs counter to immigration law, the future isn't accommodated within that law. Their simple duty was to follow the only path open to them, a path they had no power to alter. That path was risky but not overly dangerous and thus upheld their foremost duty to survive, even if it temporarily traded some happiness for unease.

With help from other illegal immigrants, Loh found a willing cargo driver and paid him a lump sum on the condition that he take Layka safely to England. Loh knew, of course, that no such guarantee was possible. Even so, he wanted the driver to promise at least once that despite the odds, he would transport Layka to England unscathed. He needed to know there would be no further news of a loved one's death.

In the early morning a week after the deal was struck, Loh and Layka arrived at the appointed spot. Loh handed Layka the rest of his money as she entered the truck's cargo section. Heads together, they promised each other that he would soon follow and that nothing could separate them after that. I don't know what they actually said, of course; perhaps these words were how I imagined a farewell between Jae and me. Not an irresponsible *Sorry* but something more honest, more elemental, like *Nothing can separate us* and *We mustn't quit but endure until we're together again.* Was this the conversation I longed for?

The truck left and Loh was alone again. Fixed in a lonely pose that had become familiar despite himself, he watched until the truck disappeared from sight. He even wondered, as he had during his early morning ride on the Euroline bus in December 2007, if he was still alive.

Loh turned to look back several times on his way home that day.

~

I leave Loh's apartment and return to Pak's. Unhooking an earring at the bathroom mirror, I feel another presence behind me and know instinctively that *It*—the one who gauged the temperature of my heart, the one who sang me to sleep—is here.

I turn slowly. *It* looks up at me and I squat down. "It was you," I whisper—the wretched ear who, having lost its partner, goes about collecting the stories of lonely, incomplete people. I extend my hands and scoop it up the way one does clear water from a well and hug it to my bosom. It wouldn't hurt to make a confession now that I was never able to before. Like a child blowing into a seashell, I put my lips close to *It* and whisper that I love him, that I knew this from the first time we met and have never doubted it since. Jae laughs faintly in response.

Somewhere along the way, the imagined ear has become a cell phone, and I put it against my right cheek. I haven't pressed his number, so of course there's no signal, no transmission to a street corner or dark apartment in Seoul. My confession hasn't been generated. But I make it anyway. I want to hear from him that we held back words of love for each other because neither of us believed in unbridled happiness, perfect fulfillment, or a moment of bliss. We looked instead for a state of constant emotional want, of unquenchable longing. I'd reply that my flaws have led me to value your existence more and that although our past may lack a burning kiss, like a romance film with the passion edited out, my empathy and yearning to be there for you became the reason for my work and my life.

I flip my phone closed. The wretched and lonely ear comes into my heart at that moment and whispers, *What was that?* Could it be that our time together isn't over yet?

December 24, 2010. Friday

Pak contacts me in a week, sooner than I predicted. We meet at Place Royale, then pass by City Hall, the Royal Museum of Fine Arts, the Museum of Musical Instruments, the Mont des Arts, and Les Galeries Royales Saint-Hubert, all popular tourist attractions. The streets bustle and the air crackles with festivity. Firecrackers burst among the cascade of night lights, laser beams dance on nearby buildings, strains of Christmas carols float in from near and far, restaurant and bar employees dressed as Santa Claus solicit passersby, and everywhere you look are jingling bells, reindeer, and baby angels with plump cheeks. On Rue des Bouchers, Pak and I enter a small pub. He orders beer; I order coffee with rum. Pak breaks the silence by commenting that I seem gaunt. I can't respond: a need to apologize has hung over me since our last encounter, yet the words stick in my throat.

"You seem like you want to apologize." His astuteness startles me. "I'm an old man, Kim *chakka*. Do you know what that means? It means emotions are a luxury. With my time growing short, I just become that way. Call it generosity or resignation."

Our orders arrive. Pak takes a sip of beer, then removes a folded piece of paper from his wallet and hands it to me. Even before opening it, I know what it is: the third and final stage of my journey from the initial L. to Loh Kiwan. First was that sentence in the magazine, then the copy of Loh's autobiographical essay. And finally, this. The reason I came so far, after all, was to meet Loh. As I continue to stare at the scrap of paper, Pak explains.

"Directions to the Chinese restaurant in England where Kiwan works. He and Layka work there together, just as they did in Brussels. Don't you need this?"

"You want me to go see him."

"I don't want anything. I'm an old man."

I find it funny that he keeps stressing how old he is and burst into laughter. He remains impassive.

"But why now, after all this time?"

"It seemed to me that preparing to meet him was more important for you than the meeting itself. You seemed to need time. Am I wrong?"

I answer with silent reflection. Is he telling me that meeting him was part of my journey to meet Loh? The thought sinks in and resonates. For a meeting between strangers to become meaningful, the two parties must engage each other's life. By traveling to Brussels, reading Loh's essay and journal, and following his footsteps, Loh Kiwan's life is now part of mine, inseparable from who I've become. It's time now for me to show Loh how encountering his life has changed mine. I need to get as close to him as he got to me. I utter his name, Loh-Ki-wan. The full name, not the initial L. that led me spellbound into a new world where I could reflect on my own life. The full name belongs to a living person who, though guided by larger-than-life questions and convictions, I might also entertain with trivial things.

"I have one more story to tell. Interested?"

Pak asks this as I finally overcome my hesitation, grab the memo, and stash it in my wallet. I look up to see that his face is flushed, perhaps from the beer.

"Yes, very."

"It's about that liver cancer patient again. Perhaps you're tired of it by now."

"Not at all. Go ahead."

I straighten and look into Pak's eyes. This will be his last statement about his wife.

"One day she asked me for a new prescription from the hospital. She was at home then, relying on painkillers after we'd given up on the anticancer treatments. We were having all kinds of struggles—help me die in peace, no I can't, please do it, my oath forbids it, etcetera. Anyway, there was no one else to pick up a new prescription for her, so I left home and started on my way. It must have been instinct. I was about to hail a cab and got a strange feeling, then turned and bolted for home. I never ran so fast in my life."

Even my breathing waits for him to continue.

"My wife . . . she was dressed as if to go out and stood leaning against the balcony rail. It's the apartment where you're staying now. She already had one leg over the ledge. Her deteriorated condition, with bones so weak she couldn't climb stairs anymore, had slowed her enough that I reached her first."

"And that's when you decided?"

"Perhaps."

"She would have felt great pain falling from that height."

"Kim *chakka,*" Pak begins, and looks at me calmly. "I do believe in miracles, since you mentioned it before. I've witnessed several of them myself. What I don't know is how to protect a patient while waiting for a miracle that happens only rarely. As you know, miracles . . . the very idea means they don't happen most of the time."

I nod until my neck hurts, the only thing I can think of doing for him. His face remains unreadable as he gazes at me. Then he turns and looks out the window. "They look good," he murmurs after watching for a time. "It's Christmas Eve, after all," he adds.

I follow his gaze to a spot outside the pub's glass door, where a young couple are kissing. Such a loving gesture goes even better with Christmas Eve than Santa Claus or carols, it occurs to me. Is Pak, too, thinking of Loh and Layka at this moment? A faint smile ghosts across his face. I realize then that Pak is thinking not of Loh and Layka but of a time forty years ago when he headed to France without money or much of a plan. He had all he needed: a young wife who trusted him completely. Pak, the poor foreign student, and his wife, a restaurant waitress and cashier at a supermarket, walked along the streets of Paris at dusk that Christmas Eve, discussing miracles that seldom happen. It was the olden days, when goals and choices were clearer: a diploma, a stable job, a good future for children both planned and already born, a small yard suitable for a barbecue, tickets for annual visits to Korea. Perhaps these mundane milestones were their own kind of miracle.

Three months after seeing Layka off to England, Loh followed. He didn't notify the authorities and didn't obtain a tourist visa allowing him to stay more than six months in a fellow European Union country. No wonder: Loh didn't go there as a visitor or tourist. He went there to live, to be lonely no more. Since refugee status doesn't apply across national borders within Europe, his departure for England meant giving up the status granted him by the Belgian government and with it, the social benefits and sense of stability he could have enjoyed as a settler in Belgium. All this to become an illegal immigrant once again, to return to a life without guarantees. No authority would prevent or even discourage a refugee from leaving and, indeed, may tacitly hope the refugee does. Loss of status means the granting country no longer has to pay for support.

Loh knew all this and left nonetheless. He'd have given up anything for even the momentary fulfillment of being with the one he loved. He knew that as long as this person accompanied him, being illegal wouldn't matter: never again would he face a cold winter alone, walking aimlessly with nowhere to go. Never again would he let a roll of the dice decide his next move.

"Would you . . . like to have supper with me? I cook."

The lie about my cooking doesn't matter. What I want to give Pak isn't food that's guaranteed to be bad but the time we'll spend eating together. The wooden table, the aromas of food, a soft voice asking to pass the sauce or salt, unhurried hands offering a dish, the slosh of water going into a glass, gentle voices mulling the events of today and the plans for tomorrow, appreciative gazes toward each other . . . and as Pak himself said, it's Christmas Eve. Glory to God and peace on Earth. Every creature on Earth deserves to share a hot meal today.

Pak looks puzzled. I get up from my chair and put on my coat. "It's Christmas Eve, after all," I prod.

"Sounds good," he answers, finally understanding my intention. We leave the pub and join the festive crowd. The streets overflow with joyous couples and families, musical quartets, and teenagers who laugh with a hint of mischief as they set off firecrackers or break empty bottles. As we walk, Pak asks in his usual tone why I wasn't surprised that the liver cancer patient was his wife. I smile quietly without turning. I don't have to see Pak's face to know he's smiling too. For the first time since arriving in Brussels, I don't feel cold.

December 30, 2010. Thursday

You must be on radiation—it must be painful. Do you look at yourself in the mirror? When will you be discharged? Anything you crave? Your right ear is with me now and doing well. I'm sorry . . .

I come across my box of medications and ponder what to do with it. In the midst of my bemusement, my laptop beeps that an e-mail has arrived. I stop packing, fetch it, and open my inbox.

It's from Yunju.

With trembling hands I move the cursor and open the attached file. A photograph fills the screen.

She still covers her right cheek with hair, so I can't see the missing ear. She probably poses this way out of consideration for me. At the bottom of the picture, a photoshopped caption reads, "Photo by Ryu Jae." I imagine Jae visiting the hospital on a clear winter day and Yunju scurrying to tidy her hair, looking repeatedly into the mirror and calling "Just a minute!" The photograph captures the moment Jae tells Yunju to smile—the shy grin on her face and the *V* she makes with her fingers as the shutter clicks.

I caress the computer screen with my right hand, feeling the warmth and soul Jae injected into this photograph.

Time now for my reply.

I take out my cell phone, open a folder, and press Yunju's number. While it rings, well-rehearsed sentences, constructed for this moment alone, load onto my tongue. I'd dutifully gathered them while reading Loh's journal, while walking the streets of Brussels, while spreading jam over toast, or while taking a shower, and now they roll into place in my mouth. Was I worried that excitement or impatience would prevent me from saying what I really wanted? Enough of that! This self-involved avoidance of her has to end. No longer will I succumb to this plague of inner pains and imaginings, conceived to protect only myself. Time now to be honest, at least with Yunju.

The phone clicks as someone answers. Knowing the call is from me, Yunju speaks first.

"How are you, Unni?"

Hearing her voice, it happens again. I place my hand over my mouth and nod frantically, as if willing the words I practiced so diligently to issue forth. But they won't. Just then, the right ear, that strange companion who has listened to so many of my stories, announces itself with a twitch. I swallow the last of my self-indulgence and grab the phone tightly with both hands.

Silence. This is the moment I've waited for.

"I'm sorry Yunju. I'm so sorry."

Did she hear me? "Unni," she begins, and my knees grow weak at what she says next. Her words, too, seem rehearsed, as if she had to say them over many times. I get up and make my way to the window. When I open the blinds, sunlight streams in and stings my eyes. Yunju repeats her question.

"Unni, did you hear what I said? Hello? Do you hear me?"

"Yes, every word. How could I not. It's this December morning sun—so refreshing and full of life. I guess this is how the city is sending me off."

Yunju starts to cry.

"It's okay, Yunju. I'm fine, really."

Time slows as I tell Yunju that I now dedicate my life to helping her hear the words her missing ear can't. Please stop fighting the monster in front of you, I say. You lose even if you defeat it because the monster consumes you either way. These and other words, and the new conviction that broke through my own silence to speak them, are also my private vow to always keep and protect *It,* that inner companion that now lives in my heart and whispers in my ear.

Yunju sobs for a long time. By degrees it ebbs as I explain that I'm not writing a script for a show but something that only a person needing atonement can write. It's about my encounter with traces of a lonely person and is more like my own diary than a work of fiction. I add that although I work hard at writing, I've struggled over whether I'm entitled to write something like this. "Unni," Yunju admonishes affectionately. As always, her sweet voice makes me forget loneliness and assures me she understands my confusion and anxiety. Whatever her words might be, I'm ready to take them.

"Enough of that, okay?" she may have said.

The right ear nudges me again, whispering that this is another moment for honesty.

"Before returning to Seoul, I need to stop by London. I depart today," I tell her. "London?" "Yes. The lonely person lives there now. I have a story to tell him. And . . . Yunju?"

"What?" she asks, and in a stream of words, I tell her I'll return to Seoul right after the meeting in London, that I won't be late this time, and that I'll never avoid her because I was too late or because I wasn't there when she needed me most. Yunju giggles. She tells me she'll pick out some good photos of Jae and send them to my e-mail account.

Yunju and I laugh together and then hang up. As I return the phone to my pocket, I sense another presence and turn around. There stands Pak. Gazing down at my suitcase, he says he'll give me a ride to the airport. He hasn't driven in a while, he adds. Did he hear the entire conversation? He shows no curiosity, though he can't have missed my tears or my smiling face.

~

After arriving at Charleroi Airport in Brussels, purchasing tickets, and checking my suitcase, I still have an hour before the flight.

The boarding pass from Brussels to London indicates a 4:10 p.m. departure.

Over coffee I tell Pak about Yunju, about the cruel irony of a seventeen-year-old enduring pain enough to question one's reason to keep living. Pak nods occasionally but isn't given to trite expressions of consolation, like saying I'm not responsible for what happened to her, which I used to hear from my coworkers. He doesn't ask for details and doesn't pass judgment. He merely listens. When I'm done he offers a cautious response: "Sometimes a life concludes well through the compassion one has for others."

Departure time nears.

I pull my carry-on toward the gate with Pak. At the gate I return the key to his apartment, which had become my haven, a place that guaranteed my safety, encouraged me to write, and nurtured my will and reason to keep living.

"Are you going to say thank you?" Pak asks before I can speak.

"You keep stealing my words."

"An old person like me—"

" . . . isn't moved by 'thank-yous'?"

He smiles at my quick turnabout. It's an innocent smile I haven't seen on him before. I smile too.

"I talked to Kiwan last night. He'll be waiting for you."

"What I wrote . . . is not fiction."

"Whatever it is, it can end only after you've met him."

"You think so?"

By way of answer, he keeps a comfortable silence, so I can ponder the thought. I start imagining my first words to Loh. Pak continues after a time.

"And then you'll return to Korea."

"Would you like to return to Korea?"

"No."

"Why not?"

"I went there ten years ago. To visit my mother's grave and make sure it's being kept up. But other than that, I stayed in my hotel room most of the time. There was nothing else to do, no place else to go, and no one to see. I left them all too long ago."

Pak's smile transforms into quiet sorrow. My curiosity gets the better of me. From the first time we met, he has looked at me with such a serious and probing gaze. When I would look back, he'd turn his head, and his face would show this same quiet sorrow.

"Can you tell me now?"

Pak looks quizzical.

"Do I look like her, your wife?"

" . . . I'm not sure."

"I'd be sorry if I don't."

"Kim *chakka,*" says Pak, putting his hand on my shoulder. "I'm not your average peevish old person." We smile once again.

Pak continues. "Come to think of it, I did say once that neither of you allowed yourself a speck of generosity."

"Yes you did."

"Now I see you . . . do look like her. In small ways—the eyes, mouth, here and there. In fact, she wanted to write too. She used to tell me she wanted to be a writer."

His hand on my shoulder slips off. He steps closer, and I catch a glimpse of moisture in his eyes. His voice is unexpectedly desperate.

"May I ask you . . . a favor?"

"Of course."

"It went better than expected. It wasn't that painful. Just once, would you tell me that?"

His hollow eyes behind the thick glasses are laden with tears so deeply humane they compel me. I step closer and whisper in his ear that it didn't hurt. It was like falling asleep, a pain-free process in which one is unaware of dying.

Pak cups my head between feverish hands and caresses my face slowly, like an artist beholding a work he's just completed, or a spirit that has just left its body. I feel a lifetime in those hands.

"How you've suffered. All your life, such hardship . . ."

Hearing him say this overwhelms me. I spread my arms and take him in my embrace.

In a corner of a busy airport where the PA constantly blares in French and English and numberless crowds scurry by, Pak and I hold each other. A small aperture opens behind him, and I peek through it to watch a man pour a drug into a glass, mix it with a little liquor, bestow a short kiss and speak febrile words, and leave in an eternal parting. He closes the bedroom door, sinks onto the living-room sofa, and wraps his head in his hands. The only sounds are the detached, standardized ticking of a clock and his own raging inner voice doubting the moment's decision. I witness what he faces when he finally reopens the door—the end of a life and his own agonizing sense of loss. I hear his long, drawn-out sobbing. As the aperture closes on a last anguished wail, I see everything in exquisite detail. What I hold in my arms now is not just a physical body but all the time it lived, the things it saw, the experiences that lifted it up and beat it down. It is the full, dignified, accomplished, and now lonesome person of Pak Yunchol.

A bird with sodden wings, who couldn't take flight and risked falling to earth, remains suspended in my arms.

The embrace ends and Pak wipes his eyes and mumbles, "Now, it's okay. It's okay . . ."

Parting is all that remains. Just before we reach the gate, Pak asks me to tell Loh that he'll visit at least once before he passes away. My eyes answer him and his bid farewell.

I turn back one last time before passing through the gate.

Pak stands motionless, his look blank. I nod once but he remains still. I realize then that he isn't looking at me but at the world beyond. I know what he sees. I turn and follow my own path, and Pak, who now helps define me, remains on his.

~

After the plane is airborne and the cabin calms down, I take Loh's journal from my bag. Stashed inside one page is a Euroline bus ticket from Berlin to Brussels from three years ago. Another page holds the yellow Post-it note on which Sylvie wrote, "Knocking on Heaven's Door." Further on is a photograph of Sylvie and Loh together, given to me by Pak.

And on the last page is a folded picture I printed out as I left Pak's apartment.

The print is dim and the outline blurry, but there's no mistaking the bright smile on Yunju's face as she makes a *V* with her fingers. Absent from the photo are the tears she hides from other eyes, and my job as soon as I return to Seoul will be to comfort her with my deepest, most affectionate gaze.

I return the sheet to its spot, replace the journal in my bag, and take out the navy-blue box. Inside are a spiral-bound notebook with a blue cover, a photo album, and a Christmas card from Ellen. Fighting the effects of turbulence, I open the notebook, and with the image still fresh, start writing the scene of farewell between Pak and me at Charleroi Airport.

I complete the scene just as the plane lands at Heathrow.

Loh, this is my story. I want to tell it to you.

The Rest of the Story Not Written Down in the Notebook

It's 4:20 p.m. when I arrive at Heathrow—about the same hour I left Brussels, thanks to the magic of time zones. I take an airport express shuttle downtown and unpack at the hotel I booked.

The Chinese restaurant where Loh works is in Queensway. The largest Chinatown, not just in England but in all of Europe, is on Gerrard Street in Soho. It is busy and hip, but Loh and Layka preferred the smaller Chinatown in Notting Hill, a quiet residential area with a large park.

After a shower, I sit on the bed and open the navy-blue box again. This time I take out the photo album and retrace my journey through Brussels. A busker plays his violin near Gare du Nord. Pak, seen in profile, drinks coffee outdoors under a parasol near the De Brouckère subway station. Sylvie stands waving at the front gate of Foyer Selah. Ellen grins from her director's chair at the orphanage. Room 308 at Good Sleep Hostel. The apartment on Rue de Naples where Loh lived, Jin Shan Hua restaurant on Rue Rasson, and several dozen Christmas scenes . . . I would imagine Loh's smile as I captured those scenes, printed them out, and organized them in this album—the same bright, innocent smile as in the photo with Sylvie at Foyer Selah. When he flips through this album, will he appreciate how his two years in Brussels shaped the person he's become? Will he understand that although he had no nationality or identification card and didn't know the language, he was never a ghost?

After browsing through the album, Loh Kiwan will read the spiral notebook with the blue cover that records my winter in Brussels in 2010, the one that starts "In the beginning he was just an initial, L." and ends with "Loh, this is my story. I want to tell it to you." Driven by a sentence in L.'s interview, I went to Brussels, spent December 2010 retracing Loh's experiences there, and through that encounter came to terms with my own life. The notebook records that monthlong journey.

I close the box and lie back on the bed.

Sleep doesn't come easy. I threw away the box of sleeping pills and other medications when I left Brussels. From now on I must fall asleep on my own.

The next day I pack the navy-blue box, leave the hotel, and head for the subway station. Several stops later I exit at Queensway station and see Queensway stretching before me: its antique shops and old bookstores; its Chinese, Indian, Arabic, Turkish, Mexican, and African restaurants; its shops with dragons, tigers, and buddha statues; its pedestrians with kebabs and crepes in hand. Many of the Chinese restaurants have signs in Chinese letters. The one where Loh works, called Quan Ting Ju, is located at 42 Queensway.

I walk a while and finally see the sign, and then I'm standing across from it.

"Quan Ting Ju" is written in red. By the entrance hangs a red lantern, not yet lit but resplendent with tassels. Beside the entrance is a floor-to-ceiling pane of glass, and through it I see a man in chef's garb kneading dough next to a rotisserie oven full of roasting ducks.

I hold the box to my chest and stare at the man. He's immersed in kneading and doesn't look up. The tall white hat seems big on his head, a playful contrast to the nimble movements of his hands. With his head lowered and the street between us, I can't make out his face. He's Asian and short, but that's all I can discern.

I catch a brief glimpse of his face when he looks back, as if responding to a voice. He smiles, and across the street I smile too. From that picture with Sylvie, I already know it's Loh Kiwan. And of course I know who called him.

I step toward the street, then cross it. Soon I will meet him.

He doesn't look my way even as I arrive at the restaurant. But when I pause in front of the window, he happens to look up, just for a moment. My legs are stuck in place. Sensing something, he turns to gaze at me.

We regard each other for a spell.

Then he smiles again, like he did moments earlier. He wipes the dough from his hands onto his big apron, walks to the door, and opens it wide for me. As I reach him, Loh takes my hands firmly in his, smiling just as he did in the picture with Sylvie, and guides me inside. I'm too overwhelmed in the moment to catch his words, but I nod after hearing Pak's name.

As the door closes again behind us, a young woman appears from the kitchen. She too smiles warmly as she hurries toward us and leads me to a table.

Layka returns to the kitchen to make tea, and in front of me sits Loh Kiwan: alive, breathing, living a life he richly deserves. His life will continue.

Today, I have a lot to tell him about the initial K.

Afterword

The Novel

I Met Loh Kiwan (*Lo kiwan ŭl mannatta*) is a novel published in 2011 by South Korean author Cho Haejin (b. 1973). In 2013, it won the Shin Dong-yup Prize for Literature, a literary award granted by Changbi Publishers—known since the 1960s for its prestigious quarterly *Creation and Criticism* (*Ch'angjak kwa pip'yŏng*)—in recognition of exceptional work by up-and-coming writers and poets. The story follows North Korean refugee Loh Kiwan on a journey from his home country to find a new home in a place where he doesn't speak the language or understand the customs. His struggles come to us through his journal as read and interpreted by the narrator, variously referred to in the story as "Kim," "I," "Kim *chakka*" (the writer Kim), and "the initial K." In revealing Loh's story for us, the narrator embarks on her own journey, parallel to Loh's, to learn what drives a person to live after tremendous loss and ultimate despair. The narrator's romantic interest is Jae, producer of the TV show for which she was the lead writer. Like Kim, Jae becomes conflicted about a show that is more manipulative than honest in presenting human suffering. We also meet Pak, a doctor who ended up with Loh's journal after helping him acquire refugee status in Belgium, and eventually, we discover his deep remorse over decisions he made regarding life and death for his patients. Then there is Yunju, a seventeen-year-old girl forced to mature beyond her years through confrontations with poverty, desertion, and illness. These characters are woven into a story of hope and trust, one that asks basic questions about what it means to be human and humane.

The Ethical Turn

South Korean writers in the twenty-first century have faced markedly different social, historical, and cultural challenges from their predecessors. Increasing ethnic diversity in the new century reflects an influx of newcomers, including migrant workers from various Asian countries, North Korean defectors, and ethnic Koreans from China working and living in South Korea. Globalization has also put South Korea on the world's radar, which has given Korean writers much greater currency beyond the country's borders. And the new century, with its growing divides between rich and poor, has spread experiences of poverty in a society where wealth has long been the overriding measure of success. Literary critic Chŏng Hong-su sees these developments mirrored in some of the major preoccupations of twenty-first-century South Korean literature:[1] the helplessness of individuals forsaken by a heightened competitive climate, a concomitant weakening of community, and a boom time for apocalyptic imagination and cryptic narratives of disaster.

I Met Loh Kiwan (2011) is a cornerstone in what one might call an "ethical turn" in Korean literature. Through such literary parameters as the preoccupations and sensibilities of the characters; the use of perspective, narrative style, and structure; and the choices of detail in which to anchor the story, works embodying this ethical turn impose on the reader a mandate to identify and examine their ready assumptions, particularly about the criteria by which people divide themselves in ways that lead to suffering. The ethical impulse is one that resists stereotypes, refuses sensationalist tropes and agendas, and rejects easy, received wisdom that entrenches rather than questions interpretations of the past and present. One observes this ethical turn most clearly in works by a new generation of woman writers, such as Han

Kang, Kim Sum, and Cho Haejin, that have emerged as an alternative to the portrayals of doomsday and the cycles of despair just described: by calling on ghosts of unjust death (*Human Acts,* 2014), by restoring the physicality of the past (*L's Sneakers,* 2015), and by confirming humanity across ideological boundaries (*I Met Loh Kiwan,* 2011). Deliberately evading a neat resolution or offering an easy comfort, they lead readers to take a long and hard look at the sources and manifestations of human suffering.

And so, while Cho Haejin's novel *I Met Loh Kiwan* does tap into the deepest wound in modern Korean history—the arbitrary, fateful division of North and South along the thirty-eighth parallel—that event is not directly portrayed but instead is felt through the story's namesake character Loh Kiwan, a twenty-year-old North Korean who is seeking refugee status in Belgium. The way this novel presents a North Korean's story—as a journey relived by and reembodied in someone else and then enlarging it as a meditation on universal suffering and perseverance—renders in ethical terms a subject too commonly consumed as ideological.

Ethics in *I Met Loh Kiwan*

As Susan Sontag observes, "Being a spectator of calamities taking place in another country is a quintessential modern experience,"[2] and North Korea has been consumed as a dystopian dynasty by much of the world beyond its borders. Indeed, memoirs from defectors and scenes of Pyongyang captured on camera show a country frozen in the Soviet era and suffering from decades of poverty under the Kim family. Such impressions have helped mark the North Korean regime as a "rogue" deserving little sympathy and as a volatile test of patience among other countries, especially the United States. But does that justify making a spectacle of North Korean people and their lives? Assuming not, then what would "just" storytelling about a North Korean person look like?

To the extent that the impressions just noted tap into a strong preexisting bias against North Korea for many readers, one easily imagines them prepped to view the eponymous protagonist of the story, Loh Kiwan, as an indictment against the regime, as a representation of its cruel policies and infamous human rights violations. Plenty of movies and cartoons in South Korea and the United States support this view of the North—indeed, you'd be hard-pressed to find one that didn't. And yet, except for a simple reference to the apparent food shortage and the hard economic conditions that forced Loh and his mother to risk their lives crossing the border out of North Korea, the story does little to fulfill default biases. By avoiding this political narrative, the story also declines to advance the recent trend in popular media of turning North Korea, an actual country, society, and history, into a cartoonish cast of villains, charity cases, desperadoes, bumpkins, hapless citizens, and other species of simpleton. The story thereby refuses even tacit support for weaponizing that trend through government stance and policy.

So much talk of evil regimes, downtrodden masses, and war, especially at a moment of escalation and sabre rattling, easily obscures an important fact: the North Korean refugee crisis started in the 1990s following the end of the Cold War. With Cold War–era Communist allies gone, North Korea quickly spiraled into economic crisis, and ensuing drought and flood pushed the country close to extinction. To this day, the term North Korean "defector" is more aptly used for those who fled the country in search of simple survival than someone fleeing the regime specifically. The majority end up in China and find menial jobs as illegal workers; some end up in South Korea through brokers and help from South Korean missionaries. But a small number of North Koreans choose to go farther, to the United States and to Europe. Loh Kiwan's character, though fictional, was modeled on such a refugee, and while he does come from North Korea, the wider refugee crisis in the Middle East and Europe today looms large as we read *I Met Loh Kiwan.* The story's setting of Brussels, a hub of international aid organizations, further underscores the common conditions among refugees regardless of origin.

Set in the 2000s, *I Met Loh Kiwan* features a familiar North Korean defector—starved, lost, and helpless—but in no sense is this novel an instrument of political spin and spectacle aimed at a sympathetic but comfortably distanced reader in free and affluent South Korea. That kind of readership is exactly what the narrator had catered to with her TV show aimed at raising funds for charity cases. When she decided to game the system and push back the date of a show featuring Yunju to a more "lucrative" long weekend that promised more viewers, the intention behind it seemed innocent enough, if not exactly benevolent toward Yunju. During the extra waiting period, however, Yunju's illness turned for the worse. Consumed by doubts that her decision to delay was really altruistic, self-loathing drives the narrator to leave Korea and Yunju on a path of self-discovery. The reader, of course, is implicated in these doubts, reflections, and convictions regarding an episode in which any of us might have acted the same way, with similar results. From the beginning, readers are compelled to think in terms that go beyond the specifics of an episode, an issue, or a nationality and instead grasp the overarching humanity encompassing all of these: what does goodwill mean, what demands it of us, and what does it mean to reach beyond sympathy and become empathetic? Doing so forces sincere reflection about what one should expect of a "North Korean story."

Just as the universality of Kim's struggles extend their relevance beyond the specifics of place, person, issue, or nation, so it does with Loh's journey. And in expanding his ordeal beyond simply one of a North Korean defector, author Cho Haejin evades the temptations of an exposé on North Korean tyranny and its impact on people. One main way she achieves this is by cleverly intertwining Loh's story with those of other characters. All these others—Kim, Pak, and to a lesser degree Yunju and Jae—ponder their own fundamental questions on life and living as human beings, and both the substance of these ruminations and the substantial space devoted to them prevent them being mere distractions or accessories to the central tale of Loh. Loh thus becomes broadly relevant across circumstance, space, and generation; he becomes, to paraphrase Loh's own musings in his diary, a key to the world of other people and ways of understanding.

Then there is Dr. Pak, an ethnic Korean French-Belgian doctor with one foot in the North, where he was born and spent early childhood, and the other in the South, where he grew up but had to leave during college for political reasons. He goes on to live a life of rich experience, recalled through the filter of painful encounters with life, death, and the moral complexities they can involve. The ambiguity of Pak's upbringing, together with the profound human dilemmas his experiences and choices represent, quickly make readers appreciate the extent to which easy terms of identity such as doctor, North Korean, South Korean, Belgian, or other miss the measure and substance of a person. This difficulty in encapsulating Pak entails, by extension, similar difficulty in consuming Loh's story as being about North Korea or a "North Korean," at least in more than an obvious and simplistic sense. More specifically, Pak's struggle makes readers ponder a choice between excruciatingly painful life and peaceful death. But it is not the specific choice itself that torments Pak. Mobilizing universals once again, his question concerns the morality of a person—any person—who could make that decision for the patient: as a doctor, is he let off the hook if refusing to end a patient's suffering upholds the oath he swore to his profession? Or would that act of helping the patient die peacefully be the moral choice? Are that oath and human morality the same thing?

I Met Loh Kiwan is charged with intense emotions radiating from questions each character pursues: whether true compassion and empathy are possible and if so, what should they look and feel like; who has the right to prevent a person from dying with dignity. The ethical depth of the novel resides, in part, in how these multiple threads remain balanced, never tipping far enough in one direction to simplify the novel's commitments.

Another ethical note in *I Met Loh Kiwan* is the narrator's reenactment of Loh's journal entries—she literally follows his footsteps, walking up and down streets named in his diary, checking in at the same hostel, eating in the same McDonald's, and meeting those whom Loh had met during his life as a refugee in Brussels. She imagines what Loh may have felt in each given situation. She gets enraged on Loh's behalf when, three years later, she encounters the same cold and indifferent hostel clerk as he had. She's heartbroken at numbers appearing in every journal entry indicating how little of Loh's money remained. She understands that each diminishment of money meant not only an impending financial problem but also yet another erasure of his mother by his own hand. On the strength of her journey in Loh's footsteps, the narrator knows that Loh was both burdened and motivated by the extent to which his mother sacrificed herself for him, first by escaping North Korea; then by working multiple jobs to hide and feed Loh; and finally, after she got killed, by a relative's sale of her body to a medical school in exchange for money for Loh's future.

At times, Kim confesses her inability to put herself through exactly the same experiences that Loh had—for example, eating a slice of bread while hiding in a bathroom stall in McDonald's. Despite the failed attempts to reenact and relive such experiences, the attempts themselves bring the narrator an acute awareness of Loh's perspective, which Meretoja deems "a necessary condition for moral agency."[3] It helps her grasp that the impossibility of perfectly understanding the other is itself a basis and argument for striving to do so.

Ethical concerns also resonate in the very plot and structure of the novel in its indirect, mediated, and cautious unfolding. At no time do all the characters meet in one place: Loh Kiwan appears only at the very end, and by the time Kim arrives in Brussels to find Loh, Pak's own meeting with him was already three years earlier. The "buildup" for Kim to finally meet Loh is itself a winding road. Pak and Kim meet to talk about Loh, but their conversations are almost never about him. Instead, Pak and Kim are each wrapped up in their own preoccupations, and conversations between the two are often cryptic and resistant to easy or default consumption. These "delays" create ample room for characters and readers to deliberate the moral conundrums presented along Kim's journey. The long and arduous wait prepares readers before they finally do meet Loh Kiwan and tells them that this should not be an easy trip. True compassion for others should not be imagined as a quick or easy process, the novel tells us.

Finally, there's the humane ethics of the act of writing itself, vested in this story with the power to save lives; heal deeply wounded souls; and build profound, lasting bridges between people whose surface identities, if mistaken for the real thing, would probably have kept them apart. Most obviously, writing rescued both Kim and Loh from depths of self-loathing that included thoughts of suicide. Her journey toward redemption and renewed health begins when she tells herself and the people around her that she's heading to Brussels to write. Loh, meanwhile, kept a diary not only to keep track of his days and to remember street names but, more fundamentally, to verify his existence even if—perhaps especially if—that existence seemed to hold no significance for others. This diary also saves him during the refugee application process when it provides crucial evidence of his identity as a North Korean.

And of course, it is Loh's writing that connected Pak, Kim, and Loh and guided each to gain understanding of and perspectives on each other. Loh's journal entries, in turn, are rewritten in Kim's own notebook. Rather than appearing as raw materials in the story, they instead serve to manifest empathy and understanding in the heart of the narrator and, through her, the reader. Loh's days of loneliness and despair, broken by a few rare but poignant joys, are thus never just words or descriptions. From the title on the front cover all the way to the end, this novel deals with "hot" ideological and political issues: North Korea, the refugee crisis, ending life with dignity, the commodification of individual suffering, and obscenely commercialized media. The achievement of *I Met Loh Kiwan* lies in addressing these potential flashpoints, not as a political stance but through living, breathing, flawed, profoundly human characters animated by inner conflicts and struggles. Its cautiously optimistic but open ending—Loh is once again an illegal refugee; Kim will now have to face what she ran away from—says that the moral of this novel lies not in its resolution but in the process, including the reading. It is the act of questioning, along with Kim, Pak, Jae, Yunju, and Loh Kiwan, the true meaning and function of compassion and inquiring how, in its truest universal form, it rises above the easy identity markers that so often separate us.

Notes

1. Chŏng Hong-su, “Sesang ŭi kot'ong kwan taemyŏn hanŭn sosŏl ŭi chari,” *Ch'angjak kwa pip'yŏng* 40, no. 4 (December 2012): 33–35.
2. Susan Sontag, *Regarding the Pain of Others* (New York: Picador/Farrar, Straus and Giroux, 2003), 18.
3. Hanna Meretoja, *The Ethics of Storytelling: Narrative Hermeneutics, History, and the Possible* (Oxford: Oxford University Press, 2017), 4.

Names and Romanization

Place-names in Brussels follow French rather than Flemish or English. The Korean original uses French more often, in part because one of the main characters, Dr. Pak, lived and worked in France and uses French names as references in his speech.

Korean names for characters and places use romanization chosen by the author and the translator, rather than adopting from existing systems such as McCune-Reischauer or the Revised Romanization of Korean by the South Korean Ministry of Culture. Romanization in the afterword follows the McCune-Reischauer system as set by the series.

About the Author and Translator

Since winning the Munye chungang's Newcomer's Award for her writing debut in 2004, **Cho Haejin** *has solidified her reputation as one of South Korea's major writers, with four novels and three collections of short stories. Described as a writer of compassion and tenderness, her works highlight people pushed to the margins of society, people viewed as others* (t'aja) *by those, both within Korea and beyond, who inhabit society's presumed mainstream. She also explores the minute interconnections that weave people together even across great distances. The title story in her recent short-story collection,* Surrounded by Lights (Pit ŭi howui, 2017)*, for example, follows the parallel lives of a Holocaust survivor's son and a Korean photographer and shows how a small kindness can lead to life-altering change. In "Happiness of a Stroller," (Sanch'aekcha ŭi haengbok), winner of the Yi Hyo-seok Literary Prize, we meet an impoverished adjunct lecturer at a college, lacking job security, who finds a glimmer of hope in messages she receives from her former Chinese student. "A Parting" (Samul kwa ŭi chakpyŏl) plumbs the fading memory of an old woman who carries guilt from an unintended action earlier in life that led to someone's imprisonment. Animating this broad preoccupation with margins and connective threads is a remarkably versatile style, ranging from conventional to what some might consider experimental. An example of the latter, her short story "Death of Hong" (Hong ŭi pugo, trans. in* Asia Literary Review Issue 32, 2017*) achieves the effect of a psychological thriller* *by using fragmentary elements and a circuitous structure in which the ending scene circles back to the opening in a search for the mysterious Hong.*

Cho's works have been short-listed for most of the major literary awards in South Korea and have won several, including the 2016 Yi Hyo-seok Literary Prize and the 2013 Shin Dong-yup Prize for Literature for the novel I Met Loh Kiwan.

Ji-Eun Lee *is the author of* Women Pre-scripted: Forging Modern Roles through Korean Print *(2015) and is currently an associate professor of Korean language and literature at Washington University in St. Louis. She reads, writes, and teaches on memory and space in post–Cold War Korean literature and domesticity and travels by colonial Korean women writers. Dedicated also to the translation of literary works, she has published* Burying a Treasure Map at the U-Turn *(2014) by Yoon Sung-hee.*